Camilla Hyde's only hope of escaping back to England from the ruins of Washington in that fateful year of 1814 lies not with the invading British soldiers but with Jared Kingston, a surly English nobleman turned planter, who reluctantly rescues her from the ravages of war. With this total stranger, Camilla treks across the huge American continent to Louisiana enduring unimaginable hardships. She is willing to travel with the Devil himself if it means she can get home to her beloved England.

Hardly have they reached the South when the Battle of New Orleans commences and, once more, Camilla is thrown into the thick of battle. And it is to Jared that once more she is forced to turn for help. . . .

Camilla

Sara Orwig

MILLS & BOON LIMITED
London · Sydney · Toronto

First published in Great Britain 1981
by Mills & Boon Limited,
15–16 Brook's Mews, London W1A 1DR

Australian copyright 1981
Philippine copyright 1981

ISBN 0 263 73435 8

Set in VIP Plantin 10 on 11 pt
by Fakenham Press Limited

Made and printed in Great Britain by
Cox & Wyman Ltd., Reading

CHAPTER
ONE

ALONG dusty Pennsylvania Avenue, across the broad lawns and slanting rooftops the August sun shone hotly. The boom of cannons in the distance mingled with the steady rumble of wagons and carriages along the streets. On the second floor of the stately President's Mansion, in the Ladies' Drawing Room, Mrs Madison, the wife of the President, looked up to face the slender girl in the doorway.

'Come in, Miss Hyde; I have been writing a letter to my sister.' She smiled at her guest. 'You look lovely today in spite of the heat.'

Camilla Hyde crossed the oval room with a graceful movement. Every dark hair was combed and secured high on the back of her head; only a slight flush on her cheeks and the glitter of large green eyes betrayed her emotions. As she sat down on a yellow damask sofa she murmured a polite 'Thank you' before she stated, 'There are rumours that the British Army will be here soon.'

Mrs Madison's expression did not change. She merely shrugged. 'We have had a constant barrage of rumours. Mr Madison was awakened last night by a messenger from Mr Monroe that the enemy is in full march for Washington.' In a softer tone she added, 'I should not say "enemy" to you.'

Camilla replied quickly, 'I understand, as I pray you and President Madison understand my feelings. I care nothing for politics; I merely wish to return to my home.'

Mrs Madison leaned forward and placed her hand over the girl's. 'Of course, we do understand. We have no cause to quarrel. Mr Madison has tried all in his power to end this war.'

With a coolness she was far from feeling, Camilla Hyde asked, 'Mrs Madison, could I take a carriage and join the British? Aberdine would be with me. I feel certain there is some way I can return home.'

Mrs Madison's brow creased in a frown as she shook her head. 'I couldn't possibly allow you to do such a thing without a male escort.' Before Camilla could say more she continued, 'But when Mr Madison returns I shall ask him to arrange some way for you to go. He will know what is safe and who to contact.'

For an instant Camilla closed her eyes in relief; the long thick lashes were dark in contrast to her pale skin. 'Home,' she said softly, then her eyes opened and she clasped her hostess's hand. 'Thank you!'

'I cannot promise what he will say,' Mrs Madison declared, 'but I shall do my best. I will instruct Freeman to have your trunks sent to your room if you would like. I am having mine packed now with state papers.'

'Thank you.'

'Miss Hyde, we will have a dinner party tonight; it will be a large affair. The senior military officers and the entire cabinet have been invited and if he is in town in time, your friend Mr Searles may be here as well. Jennings is getting the house ready now. With such an assemblage someone should know a means to help you reach your objective. Because of his friendship with your father, I feel certain Mr Searles will do anything he can.'

For the first time Camilla's hopes were almost dashed. 'The British must not be as close as I thought if there is to be a dinner party.'

'We do not know yet. Mr Madison went to the Navy yard this morning to meet with several of the men to discuss the emergency. When he returns we will know the situation.'

'But I have seen so many of the militia going past . . .'

Mrs Madison spoke rapidly. 'Mr Madison has called for roadblocks to be established. I have been on the roof watching for my husband's return because I do not intend to depart without him.'

Camilla rose and stated, 'I will be grateful always to you and the President for all you have done for me.'

'My dear child, we have been happy to do what we could. Mr Madison and your father were close friends. It was the least we could do, but I am sorry your stay has been under such conditions. This is a senseless war; perhaps it will end soon. I shall do my best tonight to find someone to help in your dilemma.'

With that promise Camilla left for her room, and by mid-afternoon three open trunks occupied the centre of the floor. Gowns and capes spilled over the chairs and bed, and Camilla gazed at the garments spread on the bed.

'I shall wear the green silk dress for dinner tonight, Aberdine. And do not pack my green riding-habit.' Her instructions were interrupted by a knock on the door.

It opened and Mrs Madison's maid stepped into the room. 'Ma'am, Mrs Madison's friends have finally prevailed and she has consented to go. The British will be here within half an hour.' Her voice rose as she continued, 'We are to leave immediately! Mrs Madison told me to tell you that carriages have been brought to the door.'

'Is President Madison here?' Camilla's pulse quickened.

'No, ma'am,' the woman replied nervously, 'there's no word from the President, but we have to leave anyway. Please, ma'am . . .' her voice faded. With a helpless look she turned and left the room.

Camilla clapped her hands together. 'Aberdine, thank goodness! At last they are coming!'

The maid gathered together her mistress's things. 'Miss Camilla, here is your reticule and parasol.'

'Fustian! Put those things down, Aberdine, I am not leaving. I shall wait for His Majesty's Army!'

'Miss Camilla, you must not!' Aberdine straightened with a frown on her face. 'You cannot remain here.'

Camilla ignored the maid's protests and crossed to the

window to gaze down at two carriages below. Behind her,
Aberdine wrung her hands. 'Please, ma'am, they are leaving
right away. We shall have to depart with them. Mrs Madison
will not leave you behind.'

'She will have no choice, Aberdine. The militia has quit the
incessant drilling in the square—they are gone. I know the
British are coming and I intend to stay to meet them.'

'Miss Camilla—' the older woman clutched the folds of her
black bombazine skirt and spoke in anguish—'we cannot
remain here. Mrs Madison will do all she can for you, but you
must do as she asks now. You know that is what his Lordship
would want.'

Camilla wheeled around and demanded, 'Aberdine, do not
say "His Lordship" to me again! His Lordship is dead and
has left me stranded in this wilderness for over six months
now. I am going home, and nothing will stop me!'

'Ma'am, I beg your pardon, but I know my duty. I will stay
with you, but 'tis not right.'

'Aberdine, the first British soldiers I see, I shall ask to be
taken to their commanding officer and explain the situation.
There will be some way then for me to reach a ship for home
and get through the blockade. Now you go along.'

The maid paled, but faced her resolutely. 'No, Miss
Camilla. Soldiers in wartime are not like soldiers at social
gatherings. You dare not remain alone.'

Camilla glanced down at the carriages below. Someone was
lashing a feather mattress to one carriage. She turned to study
the woman who had been at her side all her life. After a
moment she capitulated. 'Very well, Aberdine, leave the
trunks and come.'

'Praise the saints! You will get home soon enough, Miss
Camilla. 'Tis always difficult for you to be patient.'

Ignoring the familiarity of a servant who had been like the
mother she had never known, Camilla headed for the door.
Together, girl and maid moved through the mansion.
Camilla hummed a tune as she descended the stairs. The
odour of cooking meat filled the air; sunlight was bright

through the open door at the end of the hallway. Its appearance was as cheerful as Camilla's spirits.

At the sound of voices, Camilla paused before the public dining-room with its classical interior decoration, which was a stately backdrop for the long table set with fine crystal, tall candelabra and bone china, ready for the evening. On a sideboard wine was chilled, crystal decanters of brandy ready and waiting.

Under Mrs Madison's supervision the door-keeper and the gardener wrestled with a large painting of General Washington. She was insisting, 'I will not depart without it. You must get it free!'

The door-keeper, John Siousa, pressed his weight against the frame; the wood splintered and shattered. He removed the canvas, rolled it, and handed it swiftly to Mrs Madison. She turned, seeing Camilla for the first time.

'I am sorry, Miss Hyde, but we must flee. The carriages are being readied and we have to leave immediately. They are marching this moment for the city and our militia cannot hold them back.'

She gathered her skirts, clutched the canvas tightly and headed for the door. 'Come and ride in the first carriage with me; put your maid in the second.'

'Yes, ma'am.' Camilla followed Mrs Madison through the hallway, out into the heat to see that Aberdine was safely ensconced in the carriage which held the butler and his family. Then she hurried to the first carriage; Mrs Madison sat in the centre of the seat, and beside her was an open box filled with papers.

'Please, Mrs Madison,' Camilla said, 'I shall ride in the other carriage if you do not mind. My maid is sick with fright.'

Before giving the President's wife time for a protest, Camilla closed the carriage door and rushed towards the second carriage. She halted, glanced quickly at both, then dashed back into the mansion. She hurried into a deserted room to hide until she was certain everyone had departed.

A dull quiet descended as Camilla waited through the passing hours. She stood at an upstairs window, staring at the streaming humanity. People, wagons, carriages, men on horseback and militia on foot, rushed to and fro along Pennsylvania Avenue, stirring clouds of dust in the afternoon heat.

Camilla continued the vigil as stragglers from the militia and civilians thinned, then disappeared almost totally.

The cannon ceased as the shadows grew longer. The sky darkened on the horizon carrying a threat of rain and with it the afternoon took on a yellow-hued hint of an approaching storm.

Suddenly Camilla straightened. The first redcoat of the British Army loomed in view—two men, one coatless, were mounted on horseback. Bareheaded and dishevelled, they turned and halted at a nearby tavern. Her excitement ebbed slightly as they disappeared inside.

They were gone an interminable time before they finally reappeared, mounted, and drew closer.

With eager anticipation Camilla slipped a reticule over her wrist, surveyed the packed trunks and went to meet them. She held her skirts slightly above her ankles as she descended the stairs, then halted when the soldiers stepped through the door. In a startling movement one raised his musket.

'At last!' Camilla exclaimed. 'Thank heavens you are here! I am a British subject and I have been waiting for you. Take me to your commanding officer, please.'

The men looked at each other in silence. One was clad in deerskins, the other wore an ill-fitting red coat over homespun clothing. Bearded and ill-kempt, one turned and surveyed the deserted hall behind her before his gaze came back to rest on her. 'How many of you are here?'

'I am alone . . .'

The soldier lowered his musket slowly and smiled. 'Now, our commanding officer is a long way from here yet.' He placed the musket against the wall and advanced towards her cautiously. The other man moved away, strolling into the dining-room and calling, 'They're ready for a party.'

Camilla gazed at the approaching soldier in consternation. 'I have no intention of waiting any longer. I demand that you take me to him immediately. I shall reward you well for your time.'

The soldier continued taking wary steps towards her. 'Come on now, little lady . . .'

'If you won't take me, then I shall go on foot. Who is your commanding officer?' Camilla's entire twenty years had been spent in having her desires granted, and her aggravation rose at the impudence of the ragged man before her. She marched towards the door with high spots of colour in each cheek. The man stopped, folded his arms, and blocked her path to the door.

'Step aside!' Camilla continued to the door, certain that he would obey. As she started past the soldier, his hand closed in an iron grip around her wrist.

With disbelief she stared at the grimy fingers holding her fast. 'How dare you!' she gasped. She lifted her reticule and swung it at his face.

As easily as pulling a leaf off a branch he jerked it from her wrist with a stinging snap, then flung it aside, hitting a vase on a nearby table. The small vase toppled and fell to the floor, shattering into pieces. 'C'mere,' he growled and lifted her roughly into his arms, causing her to flinch from his foul breath.

A rage swept through her at such disrespect. In vain Camilla pounded him with her fists as he carried her into the dining-room to join his companion. The other soldier was drinking from a decanter of brandy; the fine cut-glass was lifted to his greedy mouth.

The first knot of cold fear touched her as he consumed the contents, then sent the sparkling crystal sailing through the air. The bottle hit the window and shattered the pane.

'Have a tot,' the ruffian urged his companion, motioning towards the decanters.

In desperation Camilla suddenly went limp and closed her eyes. 'Fainted, she has,' her captor grumbled.

She was dropped unceremoniously on to the floor and it took great effort to keep from crying out at the fall. She pretended unconsciousness for a few seconds, then gazed cautiously through her lashes at the men.

Both were engaged in drinking, and she feared she would never have as good a chance to escape. With cat-like quickness Camilla leapt to her feet and ran. It was the first sheer terror she had ever known.

Instantly the soldiers yelled and sprinted in pursuit as she raced from the room for the open door. Just as she neared it a grumble sounded behind her and hands caught roughly at her shoulder, spinning her about. A shrill scream of fear ripped from her throat and reverberated in the empty house.

Without warning, the soldier raised his thick hand and slapped her viciously. Her head snapped sharply on her slender neck as she struggled with him. The world was a haze of pain and rough hands; she squeezed her eyes shut tightly at his hated visage.

'Get her away from the door,' the other man hissed.

'Come he . . .' The man's words were cut short, ending abruptly in a strange gagging noise. The cruel fingers around her arm loosened and fell away.

Camilla opened her eyes and was transfixed, staring in shock at the point of a sabre protruding through the soldier's chest. Her eyes widened endlessly, unable to grasp what she beheld.

A shadow moved; a tall man clad in a white open-necked shirt and leather breeches filled the doorway. Below dark brown hair his slate-grey eyes looked deadly, filled with a cold fury.

The remaining soldier leapt for the musket leaning against the wall. The stranger kicked his hand to send the weapon sliding across the floor, and the two locked in combat.

While they fought Camilla backed away, staring at them in horror. The men crashed against a delicate velvet chair, and the legs splintered under their weight. She felt caught in a nightmare, and fled for the stairs with only one driving thought—to get away from the violence.

Before she had climbed a dozen steps she heard footsteps behind and a hand closed over her arm. She gasped when she glanced around.

'This way. It won't be safe here.' The stranger spoke with a quiet urgency.

She gazed at him while her mind was numb with terror. She could not think rationally; she felt only a desperate longing to get away. Without a word she yanked her arm to free herself from his grasp, but he held tightly and insisted, 'Quick, the British may arrive any minute. We must get out.'

The words came as if from far away; her voice was strange in her ears. 'I am British . . .'

'You cannot remain here!'

She looked into the dark-fringed grey eyes which swam before her face and then were gone. The world faded in an enveloping blackness, and Camilla Hyde fainted for the first time in her life.

When consciousness returned she opened her eyes and stared about without comprehension. The first thing she was aware of was being held close to someone; strong arms were comfortingly about her. She stirred slightly and peered up through the dusk. She was in the arms of an utter stranger, a handsome man with a firm jaw and finely chiselled mouth.

He knelt on the ground, holding her close, his attention elsewhere. Everywhere was noise that she could not fathom; shouts, explosions, glass tinkling. There was a faint odour of leather about the man; it was mingled with a smell of smoke in the air.

A shrill scream sounded in the distance, a jarring disonnance which brought memory to Camilla. She pulled away in embarrassment, causing the man to look down at her.

'Ah . . . better now?' he asked.

'Where are we?' she stammered in confusion as she glanced around and saw only the dense foliage of lush summer shrubs.

'We must cross the lawn and get away from here, but I waited until you could stand because we'll have a greater opportunity if I do not have to carry you. Will you be able to walk on your own?'

She nodded without altogether understanding what was happening. He did not hesitate, but replied, 'Good; move as rapidly as you are able.' He straightened and grasped her hand in a firm grip, then crept swiftly behind the shrubbery until they reached a point where it ended. He paused a moment and Camilla looked around.

They were close to the mansion. Another shock ran through her as she observed bright tongues of flame leaping at two windows. She tugged against him. 'It's burning! The mansion is on fire!'

Again she pulled to free herself, and was jerked roughly around. 'You cannot go in there!' he snapped.

'I have to!'

She watched in horror as a British soldier ran across the lawn with a sterling silver candelabrum clutched in his hand.

'We're leaving now!' The stranger held her wrist firmly and sprinted across the lawn past the hen houses and stables, pulling her behind him.

There was no chance to argue further; she had no choice but to hold her skirts with her free hand and struggle to keep pace behind him.

They left the lawn, crossing a lane, then turning down another one. They ran until she felt as if she would drop. Doors in buildings stood open, mute testimony to desertion by owners. Suddenly he pulled her through one of the doorways into a darkened, empty candle shop. An abandoned container of tallow and a knife indicated that the chandler had fled in haste.

He paused inside the door, allowing her to lean against the wall to catch her breath. The dark hair which Aberdine had so carefully dressed had come loose, and soft black curls pressed damply against the back of her neck. Her heart thudded loudly from the run and her bosom heaved.

The man closed the door until it was open only a crack, then continued to gaze steadily through it. The sound of hoofbeats and male voices rose, then fell. The stranger turned and looked over her head through the small-paned window at the passing soldiers until they were gone from view.

'We must find horses,' he whispered, with his chin close enough above her head that she felt his breath against her hair. She looked up to meet those grey eyes fixed sombrely on her.

'I'm Jared Kingston,' he said.

She stared at him a moment, then replied slowly, 'Thank you for saving me from ... those men.' She added, 'I'm Camilla Hyde.'

He nodded, then stared over her head again at the window. She ran a hand across her brow. The numb shock she had been cushioned in began to fade, and for the first time she noticed a throbbing in her temples. Jared Kingston looked down at her again. 'Do you have family here?'

'No,' she whispered, matching his low tones.

'What were you doing alone at the President's mansion?' he asked curiously.

'I have been visiting there.'

A commotion sounded outside and Jared Kingston shifted his attention to the window. Camilla saw a band of noisy men turn into the lane and pause before a shop. One of them tossed a rock through a window.

The memory of the soldier's rough hands grasping her arm came back clearly and Camilla shivered. Jared glanced down at her and spoke quietly. 'We should get away from the door.'

She inquired fearfully, 'Should we leave while they are some distance away?'

He shook his head. 'It would be far too dangerous on this narrow lane, because one of them would be bound to catch a glimpse of us. No, come with me.' He moved through the dark narrow shop, which was filled with shelves of candles and containers of tallow.

The back room was tidy, dark and windowless, with no outside exit. Camilla's fright mounted as the sound of the rowdy male voices grew louder, and more glass shattered somewhere outside, causing her to jump. She glanced up at the calm man beside her, wondering how he could remain so collected when they were caught in a trap.

He withdrew a flintlock pistol from the waistband of his dark leather breeches, looked around, then took her hand to pull her into a corner behind high wooden shelves which were filled with stacks of crates. He stood in front of her, poised and waiting with the pistol drawn.

Her eyes adjusted to the gloom. It was stuffy and airless in the small space and the noise outside increased. Camilla gazed up at the man so close to her and gained a degree of comfort from his presence; his broad shoulders reassuringly blocked any sight of the aisle. He stood close enough that she was almost touching him; his dark brown hair curled low on his neck, thick against his white cambric shirt.

Glass shattered and tinkled on the boards and coarse shouts rent the air. Camilla inhaled deeply and stared at Jared Kingston. There was no way for one man to hold off a mob; the plundering men sounded right at hand and wreaking havoc in the front room only a few feet away. Boots scraped on the floor, scuffling noises were heard, and Camilla knew that at least one man was in the back room with them.

Jared Kingston did not move a muscle while the man walked about, then the steps receded. Her view was blocked by the packed shelves and Jared, but the shouts and thumps coming from the front of the shop indicated riotous drunkards bent on destruction. Suddenly the noise faded and was gone.

Jared turned and clasped her hand. 'We have to get out,' he stated simply, but the moment he moved away Camilla saw the flickering reflection of orange, and realised that the shop was on fire. In the opposite corner the crates crackled with flames which blazed and spread, emitting a searing heat.

They rushed past the fire and through the wrecked shop, then halted at the entrance. The men had disappeared inside another doorway farther along the lane; only their noise revealed that they remained in the area.

Together they slipped from the shop and raced along the lane to turn into another one. A gust of wind slapped at their faces; whipping around the corners, it was hot and dust-filled. The sky darkened with gathering clouds which were low and wind-filled, rolling swiftly overhead.

At the end of the lane where the shops curved in a sharp turn, a black horse, bridled but unsaddled, trotted into view, its eyes rolling wildly. Jared Kingston breathed a soft, 'Thank God,' and quickened his step. Camilla followed, watching him draw near to the skittish horse and speak softly, all the time approaching him with outstretched hand until he could finally touch the big animal. He patted the sleek neck, fastened his hands in its mane, then caught the trailing reins.

Jared vaulted on to its back before he motioned to Camilla to come closer. He leaned down and lifted her easily on to the horse in front of him, turned and urged the animal down the lane.

Within minutes they were cantering away from the shops and houses into a violent wind; branches cracked and split loose from the trees, leaves tumbled through the air. Camilla turned her head towards Jared to prevent the dust from flying into her eyes. Thunder in the distance rumbled in an incessant dull roll.

They finally reached a grassy knoll a sufficient distance away from town; with the storm, dark had come early and night was upon them. Jared let the horse slow to a stop, then jumped down. His strong hands closed about Camilla's waist and swung her to the ground. 'I think we are safe here, for a time at least.'

Camilla turned to look in the direction from whence they had fled and gasped with shock. 'Look at the city!'

The vast blackness of the night sky above them changed in the distance; over Washington was an orb of glowing orange from the burning town. Lightning streaked the sky and the first big drops of rain fell.

Camilla stared at the burning city. 'How ghastly!' she breathed.

'Do you have relatives there?' he inquired.

She shook her head and replied, 'No.'

'Why were you alone at the mansion?'

'Mrs Madison and the servants left in the middle of the afternoon.'

'That late? I would have guessed they had departed yesterday or earlier.'

She shook her head. 'No, I do not feel that many people thought the city would ever be attacked. I have heard them speak of the natural defences of the rivers. President Madison left early this morning and we never had word from him, which made Mrs Madison want to remain until he returned. When they did leave I hid—they thought I was in one of the carriages—I wanted to wait for the British Army to arrive, because I've been unable to get through the blockade to return home to England.'

He shook his head. 'Women should not be alone in wartime. I would surmise that the men you encountered were deserters or riff-raff who were moving ahead of the army.'

'I do thank you, sir,' she declared.

In the darkness of early evening she could still make out his features as he glanced up at the sky. 'We are in for a storm.' Even as he spoke a few big drops splattered; they were cold where they fell against Camilla's skin. Jared frowned at her. 'Where can I take you?'

The last hours had been so filled with terrifying happenings that she had not given a thought as to what she would do. For the first time she realised the precariousness of her position. 'I cannot say,' she replied honestly. 'I might go to Georgetown, to one of Mrs Madison's friends.'

He shook his head grimly. 'No, I'm not riding back into that inferno and risking both our lives, only to find a deserted house.' His voice sounded angry. 'We could search for the next week for Mrs Madison and still be unsuccessful.' He hesitated a moment, then asked, 'Do you want to travel with me?'

Camilla blinked rapidly at the suggestion, and irritation rose inside her. 'Indeed not! I shall stay right here.'

He replied drily, 'You might find yourself in the midst of a battlefield come morning.'

Suddenly all the kindly feelings she had experienced towards him for rescuing her evaporated. Her indignation rose at his ungallantly blunt manner. 'I shall remain in Washington,' she replied haughtily.

He made a small bow. 'Miss Hyde, it has been—interesting. I wish you good fortune.' He turned to pat the horse's neck, and once again vaulted on to the animal's back with a lithe movement. Then, as if the heavens conspired with him to add to her discomfort, the rain became heavier.

Camilla stared in horror. 'You cannot leave me stranded here!'

He regarded her in silence which infuriated her. She had never had to ask a gentleman, or any other man, for favours. All had been at her beck and call. Now he was leaving her with the choice of being deserted on the edge of a war-torn city, or forcing her to ask him to take her along.

She asked between tight lips, 'Where are you going?'

Her anger increased at his sardonic reply. 'Does it really matter?'

She took a deep breath as they stared at each other. He turned the big horse to ride away. 'Wait!' she cried, feeling a surge of fury that she would have to rely on such a rogue. All gratitude for what he had done fled. 'I want to come along.'

He made a motion with his hand for her to come nearer. She glared up at him as he leaned down and once again swung her up before him, only this time there were no bands of rowdy marauders at their heels, no flight for their very lives. For the first time she was fully aware of his closeness, of the warmth of his arm which held her securely against him, of his breath against her hair, and her back pressed against his broad chest.

The rain fell then in earnest, pounding against them. Jared turned the horse to ride under the shelter of the trees as much as possible. 'This will put out the fires,' he remarked.

'I pray it is in time,' Camilla said.

The branches bent under the violence of the wind, causing the leaves to flutter with a soft whistling. Within a short time the storm had passed them. When it ended the horse moved at an easy pace and it was possible to converse, except that Camilla would not look up at him when she knew their heads were close to touching. As her awareness of him as a man increased, so did her discomfort at the situation.

'Since I elected to travel with you, would you perchance reveal our destination?' she asked in icy tones.

With a touch of amusement in his voice he replied, 'I shall leave you wherever you choose along the way. I suspect you will prefer the first inn we find; then you can send word to your acquaintances in Washington to come fetch you.'

She half-turned in anger to peer through the darkness at him, temper overcoming her timidity at his closeness. 'I do not have any person to send word to, except Mrs Madison, and she may have left the city. I have no idea where to reach her!'

He sobered quickly, his voice deepening. 'Surely there is someone . . .'

'There is no one,' she snapped. 'Due to the unfortunate circumstances, a sudden illness resulting in the death of my uncle, I have been stranded, unable to get through the block-ade to return to England and home. I thought if I remained behind today, when they said the British were coming, that I could find an officer to get me to a ship.'

'You little fool,' he murmured softly.

'I beg your pardon, sir!'

'Miss Hyde, if I have to endure your company, at least do not be a tiresome female,' he remarked in scathing tones. 'There must be some place you can go.'

'How very much indeed I wish there were!'

They rode in silence, Camilla's temper rising at her predicament. When he finally spoke it was slowly, as though he was thinking aloud.

'Perhaps I can get you home to England.'

She turned and stared at him. 'How would it be possible?'

There was another pause, then he said, 'It would mean that you will have to come with me now, though, and I do not think you will want to.'

'Mr Kingston, you have not informed me of your destination, and why would I not care to do so?'

'I have two ships coming in, unaware of the changing conditions at home. The British are tightening their blockade of New Orleans; I must reach a point along the Gulf to warn them, but it means I shall have to travel across country as rapidly as possible.'

Her spirits surged. 'Do you mean I could sail home on one of your ships?'

'Yes, later. These are arriving—it will be some time before they sail, but in due time I can find a way, either on my ships or someone else's, for you to return to England.'

She sighed heavily, forgiving him momentarily for the aggravation he had just caused her. 'I will go, sir. Most certainly I shall try not to be a "tiresome female".'

'I have a suspicion, Miss Hyde, that you have no conception of what you are promising. I have to reach the coast in what I hope will be little more than thirty days.'

'Thirty days!' burst from Camilla and she twisted to face him.

'That is correct. I can take you this moment to a nearby town, to an inn. It should not take long for you to find Mrs Madison.'

Camilla was caught in a dilemma. Thirty days' travel with

an utter stranger—or another indefinite wait? She had waited
so long, to no avail, during these last months. She answered
softly, 'I shall go, and I will not be burdensome.'

'Understand clearly,' he warned, 'I shall go as straight as
possible, across mountains and through wilderness, some of
which has never seen a human. There may be wild animals,
terrible weather, highwaymen and God knows what else. I
cannot coddle a delicate miss whose most rigorous moments
have been at balls and hunts.'

Camilla's eyes grew round in the darkness and she clamped
her jaw shut tightly at his insufferable attitude. Never in her
life could she recall being addressed in such a manner.
Inwardly she fumed, knowing she was absolutely helpless.
She did not want to depend on him for anything, yet circumstances had forced her to, and if she refused his help she
would be deserted in a wilderness. She answered frostily, 'Mr
Kingston, I would travel with the Devil himself, if it meant I
would get home to England.'

He did not answer, but turned the horse deeper into a
wooded area. The sound of rushing water could be heard, the
splashing a welcome invitation. Even after the rain it was a
muggy night and Camilla longed for a cool drink, but at the
moment she preferred acute discomfort to asking him for
even the smallest of favours.

The horse headed straight for the water, and as soon as it
halted and lowered its head to drink Jared Kingston swung
his leg over its back and dropped lightly to the ground. He
reached up and lifted Camilla down. She had supposed when
they stopped that they would drink as well as the horse, but as
soon as he released her he remained in front of her, blocking
her from the tempting water.

With eyes adjusted to the night she gazed up into his
solemn countenance.

'Miss Hyde, I deem it necessary that we reach an understanding at the outset of this venture.'

Camilla regarded him, fully expecting an apology for his
ungentlemanly remarks earlier. 'Yes, Mr Kingston?'

'I suffer no weariness at this hour, and am in considerable haste to reach my destination, therefore I have no intention of halting at an inn for what might be another twenty-four hours at the least.'

Camilla realised she should have known better than to expect an apology from so arrogant a man. 'I can travel quite as well as you, sir. You need not fear that I shall cause you delay.' She could not help but notice his height, which she wished was not quite so overpowering.

'You may be extremely hungry and weary before I halt to rest,' he warned.

'I fully understand, and do not mind such hardships,' she replied. She was growing impatient for him to move from her path.

His voice was quiet. 'I pray so, but that is not the object of this discussion.' His voice hardened. 'There is another matter to consider.'

CHAPTER
TWO

SHE tried to speak as coldly as possible. 'Then, sir, suppose you come to the point.'

'After this night you will be compromised. You will be spending night after night alone with me, and while there will be nothing in actuality to sully what I would guess is a fine reputation, none the less you know one such night would be your ruination in England. I want this settled now because, Miss Hyde, I am engaged, and I have no intention of marrying you to save your reputation. I have saved your life and that is as far as I shall go.'

Camilla almost reeled from the shock of his arrogance. Rage enveloped her to such an extent that she quivered. Her voice was filled with emotion as she declared, 'I am beginning to think that being left alone might be far preferable. That, sir, is the most insufferable conceit I have ever encountered. My reputation will not be sullied; I can assure you I shall never breathe a word to a living soul that I have even known of your existence—and as to marriage!' She drew herself up. 'Mr Kingston, I would rather drown myself than endure such a situation. I have no intention of marrying any man, but you, sir, I can promise that I would never consent to be your wife.'

Her voice throbbed with emotion from wrath held in check, and when Jared Kingston answered he spoke calmly. 'I intended no insult, Miss Hyde, I merely want to have our situation understood clearly from the beginning. I will abide by what I say, make no mistake.'

'And I, sir, will abide by what I have stated. The first possible moment that we reach civilisation I shall part from your company.'

'I do not intend to be insulting, Miss Hyde, but I also do not propose to return to civilisation and turn around one day to stare into the drawn pistol of an angry papa.'

'Have no fear, sir, my papa has been dead for eight years, and my uncle—who was my guardian—also recently died.'

He raised one dark eyebrow and spoke coolly. 'Then that is settled and clearly understood.' He stepped to one side and motioned with his hand towards the creek. 'Care to drink?'

Without a word she swept past him and knelt a few yards away, ignoring him totally. Her hair had come unpinned; she caught it up and secured it again. Suddenly she gasped and glanced involuntarily at Jared Kingston, exclaiming, 'My reticule! It's gone!'

'You shan't need it,' he stated. He had waded into the stream and was observing her over his shoulder while the clear water swirled against his boots.

'But I have no money!' Camilla cried, an event which was unprecedented in her young life and too terrible to contemplate. He repeated his statement and added, 'I will supply whatever you need, Miss Hyde. It will not be difficult to do so; do not concern yourself needlessly about the matter.'

She stared at him, transfixed with horror in the realisation that she would be dependent upon him, physically and financially. She wrung her fingers together at such an unbearable thought.

He turned with his head cocked to one side as he studied her. ''Tis no problem, forget about it.'

'But, I have never been dependent on anyone!' she cried.

'Oh, come now, Miss Hyde, as a child . . .'

She interrupted him, saying, 'As a small child, yes, but Papa was too busy to be concerned and he taught me early in life to take care of my own affairs. I am not accustomed to relying on others, as many young women of my age do.'

All the calamities of the day, compounded and monumental to a young lady who had led a secure life with every whim satisfied, settled on Camilla like a great boulder. She closed her eyes momentarily, as if she could shut out the world and everything undesirable.

'Are you all right?' Jared Kingston inquired.

Her eyes flew open. 'Indeed I am!' she snapped, determined not to indicate weakness in front of him. 'I shall have to rely upon your generosity for the time being, Mr Kingston, loath as I am to do so, but the moment I am able to send notice to my solicitors I shall fully repay you all cost.'

'It won't be necessary,' he stated, and turned away, bending and scooping up water in his hands to splash against his face.

Tears of anger and frustration stung her eyes, but she choked them back, determined to manage the best she could with what fate had dealt her. She patted water on her arms, relishing its refreshing coolness, then she leaned forward and splashed it against her face. She was conscious of her feet being uncomfortably hot and longed to slip out of her shoes and step into the cold water, but she had no intention of committing such an undignified act in front of Jared Kingston. She caught up a corner of the blue organdy skirt, leaned down and gently patted her cheeks dry with it, then rose and strolled towards the horse.

Jared was already mounted, and he leaned down once more to lift her in front of him. Without conversation they commenced the ride, fording the stream and moving through dense trees to come shortly upon a narrow winding lane. Jared guided the horse on to the lane and they rode at a steady pace.

His arm encircled her waist and held her firmly. Camilla despised the necessary closeness, but the longer they rode in silence the more her anger dwindled until it was forgotten and replaced by a growing awareness of the undisturbed night countryside.

The muggy heat of Washington had been left behind; the earth had cooled, and a light breeze gently stirred the air. The only sounds were the clop of the horse's hooves against the ground and the constant chirp of crickets. A comfortable coolness enveloped Camilla. She was rocked lightly by the steady movement of the horse and held close against Jared Kingston. It had been a long, difficult day fraught with experiences such as she had never had, and now all was darkness and quiet. Gradually she relaxed until she began experiencing difficulty remaining awake.

Her eyes fluttered open and she stared blankly into space, coming awake to a first impression so foreign that she could not collect her thoughts. She remembered then and raised her head quickly from the warm crook of Jared Kingston's shoulder.

His voice was low and quiet, close to her ear. 'There's no need for you to arouse.'

He shifted slightly and her cheeks flamed to think that she had slept in his arms. 'I . . . I didn't realise . . . I did not intend to sleep.' She had no intention of dozing any more, but as if her body had developed a will of its own to confound her, she felt her lids droop. She straightened, and again he urged softly, 'You may as well sleep; I do not mind in the least.'

Vaguely Camilla thought how insufferable it was for him to feel that she was fighting sleep to please him, but it seemed too much effort to consider it. Her eyelids closed and she was asleep, only to waken again much later when the first rays of the early morning sun hit her eyelids.

They rode alongside another creek, this one deeper and cascading over smooth brown rocks. Jared halted the horse, dropped to the ground and lifted her down. 'Good morning,' he addressed her pleasantly.

Attempting to come more fully awake, Camilla mumbled a response and ran a hand lightly through her tangled curls.

'Are you hungry?' he inquired.

She looked up at him for the first time in the clear light of day and received a shock at the rugged handsomeness of the man. The rising sun caught glints of auburn in his thick dark hair. His grey eyes were cold, like slate, above fine cheekbones and a firm jaw. A dark bruise discoloured his cheek and a thin red cut ran from the corner of his mouth to his chin, evidence of the fight on her behalf. In their first meeting the previous afternoon at the mansion, she had been under too much emotional stress to take notice of him; now she wished he did not look so disturbingly commanding.

She made no reply, merely shook her head, and he turned away towards the creek, leaving her alone. She glanced about and saw they were deep in a wooded area on a slope. The creek bed cut a sharp winding path through the trees.

She regarded the easy swing of his long stride, knowing full well that he could have slept little, if at all, during the night. She longed for her home, for the orderly life she had always known. The thought of waking in her large feather-bed with the casement windows open above the rose garden and Aberdine moving silently about the bed, handing her a morning pot of chocolate, rose in her mind and caused a great longing to fill her being. Instead she was weary, hungry, and riding through a wilderness with an aggravating stranger.

At the thought of him she glanced in his direction. He was standing at the edge of the creek. He removed his black boots and placed them together carefully, straightened, and in a swift movement pulled his white shirt over his head, revealing a broad suntanned back with rippling muscles.

Camilla gasped and averted her head instantly. The man had no decency at all, she decided. She lifted her skirts slightly and hurried away, stepping over twigs and small stones to climb the slope and move upstream without a backward glance. A hot wave of embarrassment, matched by indignation, swept over her.

'Miss Hyde!' he called clearly.

She stiffened and answered, 'Yes?' with her back to him. Nothing could induce her to turn and face him.

'Do not wander too far away.'

'I shan't!' she replied coldly, and hurried round a crook in the stream.

She took small running steps, wanting to escape his presence completely. In a moment she halted and glanced fearfully over her shoulder as if wary of what she might discover. All she saw was a peaceful woodland scene from the early morning sun dappling the green leaves of tall oaks to the cool shade about her on the mass of low thick growth on the ground. Welcome as the view was, and the lack of seeing a robust male who displayed no trace of gentlemanly endeavour to observe the customs of polite society, the embarrassment she had just suffered was replaced quickly with a stronger emotion. Camilla's green eyes sparked with anger at being treated in such a manner.

Did he not observe any proprieties? she wondered. The men she had met during her stay in Washington had never treated her in any such way, but of course Mrs Madison had carefully supervised all introductions. No indeed, they had not displayed such coarse manners, so she could not truthfully say that all Colonials were guilty of such low conduct. She recalled that he had informed her he was engaged; somewhere in the world there was a female who was enamoured of the man. His handsomeness could never overcome such uncouth behaviour, but Camilla realised that perhaps he was not such a rogue with all women.

The thought gave her small comfort, for it meant that he took little notice of her as a female—a circumstance which was as novel as it was aggravating. She had little use for men, but she had always accepted their attention and gallantry as courtesies due to her.

She whirled, in hopes that turning her back on the direction in which Jared Kingston stood would remove all thought of him. The water was running and clear, an invitation which she could not resist.

Camilla stepped out of her shoes and let the pins out of her hair. The glossy tresses tumbled over her shoulders in soft curls, and raised her skirt to her knees and waded into the water. The first cold shock sent a shiver through her, then she grew accustomed to the temperature and waded into the middle of the stream which became progressively deeper. A large brown rock made a handy seat; she tucked her skirts neatly about her knees, then leaned to one side to allow her long hair to reach the water.

Stretching until her head was in the creek, she ran her fingers through the thick locks, then raised and wrung the water from her hair as best she could.

'Ready to ride?' Jared Kingston called.

Camilla jumped, nearly toppling into the stream. 'You startled me!' She looked up to discover him mounted on the horse at the edge of the stream.

'We can wait if you are enjoying yourself,' he stated.

'That won't be necessary,' she snapped quickly, rising and crossing to the bank. She had no intention of continuing to dabble in the water under his scrutiny. She snatched up her shoes and stared up at him as he swung her easily on to the horse.

'Two horses would be a vast improvement,' she declared.

'I agree, and the first farm we locate I shall do what I can to remedy the situation.' He turned the horse and moved slowly away from the water.

It took until mid-morning to find a farm. It had a small log cabin on newly cleared land in gently rolling hill country. A man with sleeves rolled to the elbow was wielding an axe, splitting logs with a steady whack which reverberated in the air. At their approach he stopped and waved; Jared Kingston returned the gesture.

'I shall introduce you as my wife, Miss Hyde. It will save explanations.'

She turned in consternation. 'I see no necessity for that. I think "Miss Hyde" will be sufficient.'

'Unmarried misses should not travel about the countryside. This is a new and primitive land. We shall do it my way.' He raised his voice and called a greeting to the farmer.

'And suppose I contradict you?' Her tone was icy.

They neared the farmer, who strolled forward to meet them. Before he halted and dismounted, Jared spoke under his breath, 'I suggest you don't.' He lifted her off the horse with his eyes fixed on hers in a heavy-lidded hardness that was clear as any verbal threat would have been.

Camilla's green eyes sparked, but she turned and allowed him to introduce her to Mr Jeremy O'Neal as his new wife, Mrs Kingston.

It was soon clear that there would be no horse to spare, for only one was in sight, fenced in a small enclosure close to the log house.

When they stepped inside to meet Mrs O'Neal, Camilla suffered a pang of pity at the pretty young woman who straightened from a large cauldron hanging in the centre of the fireplace over a small fire. The cabin was two rooms, clean and polished, but of simple, crudely constructed furniture. A cradle with a sleeping baby was placed near one of the open windows.

Even with the fire, the interior was pleasantly cool. They were entreated to stay and eat. The inviting aroma rising from the kettle assailed Camilla's nostrils and made her recall how long it had been since she had last eaten.

Jared accepted for both of them, and soon they were seated. Mr O'Neal discussed the difficulties of farming with Jared, while his wife continued to stand beside the cauldron and stir its bubbling contents. Camilla moved to sit close beside her and leave the men to themselves.

The women discovered mutual interests, first in books, then in fashions. To Camilla's dismay she learned that Peg O'Neal was almost the same age as she—only twenty-one, a year older. Then the baby awoke and his lusty cries filled the small home. As Peg hurried to tend to the infant, Camilla stepped beside her quickly. 'Here, I can stir, then you can take care of your babe.'

Peg O'Neal thanked her and straightened, leaving the long iron ladle in the hanging pot. Camilla reached for it and grasped a burning handle. She cried out in surprise and released it as rapidly as she had taken hold, shaking her injured fingers.

Her eyes met Jared Kingston's and she saw the amusement

in his. A hot flush rose in her cheeks as Peg lifted the baby then turned to ask, 'Are you all right?'

'Yes,' Camilla replied, wishing there was some way to cook without Jared's steady supervision. She grasped the handle gingerly by the end, finding it still uncomfortable, but at least not sufficiently hot to burn. She stirred angrily, hating Jared for laughing at her inexperience, then to her relief, both men arose. Mr O'Neal informed his wife that he wanted to show something outside to Mr Kingston, and they departed.

Camilla, whose most gruelling work heretofore had been fine embroidery, was increasingly appalled as she realised what Peg O'Neal's daily duties must be. The young mother, with the baby in the crook of her arm, offered to take over at the cauldron once again.

Camilla shook her head, imploring, 'You sit down with your babe and tell me what to do. I do not mind in the least.'

With a sigh, Peg O'Neal complied. Under her instruction Camilla cooked while the baby was fed, set the table and served up the meal. When it was ready she crossed to the door and stepped outside to summon the men.

Jared's shirt-sleeves were rolled high and he was lashing together two long poles held by Mr O'Neal when Camilla called them in.

When they began eating Camilla decided that nothing had ever tasted quite so good as the thick stew and hot bread. Jared complimented Peg on the delicious food; she smilingly refused credit, stating that the achievement was Camilla's.

Camilla shook her head. 'Thank you, but I did nothing except stir your cooking.'

Mr O'Neal laughed. 'Perhaps you are like my Peg, Mrs Kingston, and had little experience in cooking before marriage.'

'I know little about it,' Camilla replied softly.

He glanced at Jared. 'Ah, now sir, be patient.' He smiled at his own wife and added, 'A little love will make up for a few burned potatoes.'

Camilla looked up into Jared's unfathomable grey eyes, which gazed with disconcerting steadiness into her own as he answered, 'I shall remember that advice.'

Camilla felt her cheeks flush; she wished there was some way to control blushes. To change the topic she turned to her host. 'This is a beautiful spot, but so isolated, Mr O'Neal. What caused you to settle here?'

A look was exchanged between the O'Neals before he answered, 'I left the state of Rhode Island over a disagreement about a debt.'

'Oh,' Camilla said hastily, 'I did not intend . . .'

Mr O'Neal interrupted easily. 'Do not be concerned, 'tis long forgotten now. This is a pleasant place. There are Indians south of us, but we have had no trouble. We have a good view in all directions, so 'tis easy to sight anybody approaching the place.'

The conversation flowed easily while they finished eating, thanked the O'Neals and said their farewells, taking a basket of food. But later, when they had ridden some distance, Camilla returned to the subject. 'I feel I blundered today, but I had no intention of sounding curious . . .' she paused.

'When you inquired why they settled in such a place?'

'Yes.'

'Miss Hyde,' Jared replied, 'this is a new world. It is filled with men who have fled all sorts of conditions, and are hoping for a fresh start in life. You will discover it prudent not to inquire about a man's background or his reasons for settling in a particular location.'

'I never thought of that.' Camilla looked up at him. 'They seemed so nice.'

'There are some quite likeable people who find themselves in circumstances from which they would like to escape,' he answered.

Her eyes widened in surprise at the sincerity in his voice. She turned away, feigning an interest in the view ahead. Jared Kingston had not mentioned one word about his birthplace—or his past. She suspected strongly that there was a reason for the intense manner in which he had just spoken, as if he himself had done that very thing and was attempting to flee a dark past.

She blinked in contemplation of the possibility; what could he have done, she wondered, to drive him to this new land—or was it her imagination?

They rode in silence under a cloudy overcast sky which caused the air to be muggy. The work at the O'Neals' and the travel across country filled Camilla with weariness in spite of the afternoon hour.

Jared had hoped to reach a town, but when the sun finally sank low on the horizon they had not found even an indication of one, and he declared they would halt to rest.

They unpacked cheese, cold slices of venison, sweetmeats, a bottle of rum and a loaf of dark bread. Apples filled the bottom of the basket. After they had eaten and returned the left-overs to the basket, Camilla sat on the grass and folded her arms against a growing chill.

Jared looked down at her. 'Miss Hyde, we have no bedding, not even one blanket. By now you should know you can trust me. I think you will spend a far more comfortable night if I am close beside you.'

She was glad of the dusk, wishing it even darker as she felt herself blushing again. 'Thank you, Mr Kingston, but I shall manage quite well.'

He shrugged and moved a few feet away, sinking down in a quick movement to sit on the ground. He looked intently at her, causing Camilla to shift her gaze nervously.

'I don't feel it is just me,' he said softly, startling her.

'What is just you?'

'That you are afraid of,' he replied. 'Why do you fear men?'

She frowned. 'How ridiculous! I am certainly not afraid of men. I have been around men all my life. I never knew my mother—she died at my birth; my close relatives were male. If I were truly afraid of men, I never would have waited alone at the mansion for the soldiers to arrive.'

One corner of his mouth curled in a crooked smile. 'That proves nothing but your foolishness and innocence.'

'Mr Kingston! It seems you deliberately try to provoke me. Sir, I am quite weary.' She lay down on the coarse grass and weeds, crossed her feet at her ankles, and closed her eyes in a fervent hope that he would say no more.

His voice was persistent. He drawled, 'You fear me, you do not trust me, even after I saved you—and you won't allow yourself the liberty of losing your temper with me. You are all bottled up inside.'

Her eyes flew open and she stared up at the darkening sky. She snapped her eyes shut quickly and stated, 'I have no intention of carrying this discussion further, Mr Kingston. So long as I do not interfere with you, sir, my actions are none of your affair!'

'Quite so,' he answered with an infuriating cheerfulness, 'except that I cannot help but be curious.'

He became quiet and Camilla longed to peep and see what he was doing or if he was asleep, but her curiosity was overridden by the fear that she would meet again that intense grey scrutiny. As she stretched out with her eyes closed, the exhaustion she had suffered all afternoon overcame her and sleep came rapidly.

It seemed she had just closed her eyes when she was awakened suddenly to find a hand clamped firmly over her mouth.

CHAPTER
THREE

CAMILLA'S eyes flew open, but before she could struggle, Jared spoke quickly in her ear. 'Do not make a sound. Come with me quickly.'

He moved his hand away from her face and took her by the arm. She rose and rushed behind him, struggling to keep from making any noise and hating each step on twigs and hard pebbles.

They moved quickly through the trees, leaving the horse behind. Suddenly he stopped and squeezed into the thick branches of an oak; he pulled her close against him with one hand and held his pistol with the other. She stood with her head against his chest; his steady heartbeat was considerably slower than her own frightened one. She strained to listen for any noise, but there was complete silence. She reached up and touched his shoulder.

He inclined his head and she whispered in his ear, 'What is it?'

He shook his head and motioned with his hand for her to be silent. Camilla obeyed, but she was becoming concerned lest he had taken leave of his senses. She could not hear anything unusual.

The time lengthened and stretched. She was growing more alarmed over his actions than about anything around them in the night, when she heard a twig snap close at hand.

Her tense body jerked and his arm tightened about her. She felt him stiffen, then there was the faintest whisper close at hand, the words too low to be understood.

Like the barest sigh, a soft sound of somebody answering was heard, too low to be intelligible.

Camilla stared into the darkness; seconds passed and turned into minutes and still Jared would not move a muscle or allow her to.

All of a sudden he leaned down to whisper, 'I think they are gone. We will double back to get the horse.' He took her hand to pull her along behind him.

Camilla felt chilled, even though it was a summer night. The back of her neck was cold, as if touched by something dark and frightening. She hurried after him, this time trying doubly hard to be quiet. She had no idea of direction, much less of how to find the horse or where they had slept, but within a few minutes Jared came upon the animal.

He gathered the reins and led the horse behind them. Finally Camilla leaned forward to ask, 'Who was that?'

'Indians,' he replied. 'I do not know if they were friendly or not, but we could not take a chance. I am unfamiliar with this part of the country and I'm uncertain if they are hostile.'

They reached an open space and halted to mount. She looked up and could see Jared scanning the area ahead as well as around them.

All looked peaceful; they continued on their way at a slow pace to be quieter. He guided the horse along in the shadows to remain in darkness. Finally Jared spoke in a normal tone of voice. 'I am sorry if I frightened you, but it was necessary.'

She did not reply, but rode in silence, lost in her own thoughts. Now that the threat of danger was removed she could reflect on the happening. The more she thought about the circumstances the more curious she became, not so much about who was stalking them in the woods, but about Jared Kingston's ability to cope so competently with the situation.

She had not heard any sound except the one whispered exchange. How had Jared not only heard them coming, but also known when they were gone? He had moved with lightning speed and absolute silence. Any noise from their footsteps she had caused, of that she felt certain.

She thought of Lord Northolt, a London acquaintance who had escorted her to balls and the Opera. In no way could she picture Lord Northolt's moving about at night in the woods in such a manner. Her curiosity increased to the point where it overcame exhaustion. She shifted to gaze up at him. 'Mr Kingston, what is your occupation?'

He glanced down at her. 'I farm,' came the cryptic reply.

'But you said you have ships arriving, so you must also be the owner of sea-going vessels.'

'That is correct.'

His curious actions were not explained by two such ordinary occupations. He obviously was a man of some substance; the loss of her reticule seemed to him to pose no difficulty.

She had been too shocked at first, then too angry or tired to ponder much about him, but now all sorts of questions arose. She asked, 'Why were you in the President's mansion?'

He glanced down briefly, then stared ahead. 'I was merely passing and heard you scream.'

'Do you live in Washington?'

'No, I was returning to this country and arrived there first.'

'Where is our destination, Mr Kingston?'

'Ultimately—Louisiana.'

Camilla gasped. 'Louisiana!' She stared up at him in shocked horror. Their proximity on the horse caused her to be only inches away from his face, making it difficult to talk. She slid off the horse in a quick movement, turned and looked up to ask, 'Sir, can we halt to discuss this?'

'Certainly.' He pulled on the reins and gazed down at her.

'Could you have the grace to dismount, so that I do not have to converse with you in this manner?'

He nodded with a wicked flash of white teeth and dropped to the ground in front of her. Camilla struggled to contain her anger. 'Sir, I think you have not dealt fairly with me. Louisiana is across the continent. You merely said you needed to reach the coast.'

'Miss Hyde, what does it signify? The choice was to wait in some inn until the time would come when you would locate

Mrs Madison, which could be months, leaving you entirely alone without money—or to come with me. Had my destination been Bolivia, I see that it would have made little difference.'

'I feel that is dreadful, sir. You should have at least informed me and allowed me to make the choice.'

He answered coolly, 'I warned you of the conditions under which we would travel, because that was necessity. If it had meant I had to wed you to save your reputation, I would have left you at an inn. Other than such a drastic circumstance I feel you are far safer to come with me. I can get you home, sooner than Mrs Madison could, most likely, and until you discover her whereabouts you would be at the mercy of innumerable strangers.'

His tone grew colder. 'From all indications that would have been a situation beyond your ability to handle.'

Camilla seethed in helpless rage. She wanted to cry out at him, infuriated that the one condition which would have caused him to abandon her was the contemplation of marriage to her. Not only had he deceived her, but also he had been insulting. She had been taught all her life to withhold her emotions, so she turned on her heel and hurried along the lane.

He mounted, rode up beside her and swept her up before him without any warning. 'Do you have something else to add, Miss Hyde?'

'Indeed not! You know quite well how I feel, sir.'

'No feminine tears?' he asked lightly. When she did not reply he continued blithely, 'Quite a refreshing change. Perhaps it would be a little more human if you gave vent to your feelings, but then that is most unlikely beneath that cold, ladylike control you exhibit.'

She raised her chin, refusing to answer and they rode in silence. She tried to recall her lessons in geography about the French territory. Finally she asked, 'How many miles away is Louisiana, sir?'

'Slightly over a thousand, I would say.'

Her head reeled as if she had suffered a blow. 'Over a thousand! You and I shall be alone . . .' her voice faded in the contemplation of her predicament.

He sobered and replied, 'Under normal conditions, Miss Hyde, it would be a very long journey, but I warned you of my urgency. I shall break all speed records and it will be far less time than you could possibly envision. We will stop little and for very short hours; we will not halt often to eat. One can survive without regular meals.'

'But you stated earlier thirty days; we cannot cover that distance in such a time.'

'No,' he replied, 'I am heading for a place on the Gulf. Someone lives there who will be able to reach my ships and warn them before they sail into a British blockade at New Orleans. Now that the war with Napoleon has ceased, the British can concentrate on us. The move by the British towards New Orleans commenced long after these ships of mine were under way; they are coming from South America and will be unaware of what awaits them.' His voice hardened. 'I shall reach Spanish territory in little over thirty days.'

She glanced at him. 'No matter how fast, we shall still be together a long time.'

He replied in a cold voice. 'I can stop at an inn the next time we halt and you can remain behind.'

Camilla considered the possibilities and knew there was only one answer. 'I have come this far—I could not remain without money as you know. Also, you have assured me of my return home. For that promise, I will go with you.'

Silence descended between them and lengthened for more than a mile. He urged the horse to a faster pace, then finally when the animal slowed Camilla spoke, returning to the topic of their earlier conversation.

'You moved through the woods tonight with a remarkable ability that does not seem likely to have been developed by farming.'

'This is a new country, Miss Hyde. There are many

dangers, and there are still many primitive areas. One learns quickly when it is necessary.'

Why, she wondered, would it be necessary? 'You said you are engaged; may I ask her name?'

'Paulette Fourier,' he answered easily.

'She is French?'

'Yes, I suppose you would say French, although she has lived most of her life in this country. Her father owns an immense plantation near New Orleans.'

'I see.' The conversation was taking a more personal turn than Camilla cared to let it, so she inquired, 'What sort of ships do you have? What wares do they carry?'

'Various things, such as wine, iron, silks.'

'What is the name of your shipping line?'

He seemed amused. 'Miss Hyde, I am a privateer.'

She whirled to face him and exclaimed, 'You are a pirate!'

He replied with a quiet firmness, 'I am a *privateer*—it is legal. I have a letter of marque from Cartagena which gives me the right to attack and loot Spanish ships whenever I choose.' He explained, 'Many countries grant these documents, which is each country's way of sanctioning such enterprise. There are certain ports where I can dispose of the goods in a lawful manner. Usually a country will grant them against another country with which they are at war.' He looked down at her and added quietly, 'I also have a letter of marque from the United States.'

'Against whom?' she asked, suspecting what his answer would be.

'The British,' he replied confirming her suspicions. 'There are few granted by this country.'

'You are a pirate,' she declared once more.

'A pirate preys on any vessel at sea and takes everything he can get; that is not the case with a privateer.'

She studied him. 'To the Spanish and the British you are a pirate.'

He shrugged. 'That may be.'

From the frightening awakening in the woods to the

knowledge of their destination and his piracy, the night had been one shock right after another. She realised that she had entrusted her life to a pirate, but she had declared she would go with the Devil if it would enable her to get home. Jared Kingston was as close to being one as anybody she had ever encountered, yet he had saved her life and had not taken advantage of her helplessness.

She stared into the shadowy countryside. Tall oaks dotted the rolling hills, full and spreading with thick summer growth. A rabbit broke cover from high grass and scampered in a zigzag course over a rising knoll. The night was lightened by heavy grey clouds which raced swiftly across the sky and carried with them the mingled odours of dust and rain. Everywhere was undisturbed land, with crickets chirping and the steady thud of each hoof the only noise.

Camilla inquired, 'Where were you born, Mr Kingston?'

'A good distance away. Where is your home?'

'Amberley, in Sussex,' she answered, fully aware that he had not replied to her question. 'Have you been to England?'

'Yes,' he replied, 'quite a long time ago. How did you come to be so far from home?'

'My uncle has been my guardian since my father died. For the last two years he has allowed me to travel with him.' She gazed into the darkness a moment, then continued, 'When we came to this country we intended to be here only a short time, then journey to Canada, but he contracted first a back ailment, then pneumonia, and was ill for three months before he died. Because of the worsening situation between the two countries I have been unable to get home.'

She sighed heavily. 'Earlier, I would have been able to leave—the New England states have opposed the war, and it would have been possible to depart freely from there—but I could not sail and abandon him to die in a foreign hospital without any family, so I remained and was trapped here.'

'How did you come to be residing at the President's mansion?'

Camilla ran the horse's coarse mane through her fingers abstractedly before answering. 'My father and President Madison were close friends. My father spent a considerable amount of time here in the last few years of his life.'

'How did that happen?' Jared inquired.

She shrugged. 'My father had a wide range of interests. We have farms; he was interested in inventions. For a time he even owned land in this country, but he sold his holdings.'

'And your mother?'

'She died when I was born.'

They rode in silence for a few moments, then Jared continued with his questions. 'So you stayed at the President's mansion with your uncle?'

Camilla shook her head. 'No, we were at a hotel, but after he died, Mrs Madison insisted I stay at the President's house until I could leave for home. The Madisons were most kind to us from the first moment of our arrival.'

'And did this leave some dashing titled fellow languishing at home, waiting for your return?'

How could anyone be so consistently infuriating? she thought. 'Indeed not!'

He laughed softly, only increasing her agitation. 'Come now, Miss Hyde, I intended no insult by such a question. You are the right age to attract young men and, when you have the luxuries of a bath and hair brushing I am certain you are sufficiently pretty. There should be a young man waiting.'

Camilla's eyes widened in the dark. 'The luxuries of a bath and hair brushing' ... 'sufficiently pretty' ... his words clanged like a jarring bell in her mind and a hot wave of anger engulfed her, all the more infuriating because she could do nothing but sit close to him on the horse and keep still. 'There is no one,' she replied tartly.

'Ah, then that does arouse my curiosity, Miss Hyde. There must be some reason for such a void in your life.'

Camilla removed her hands from the horse's mane and knotted them in anger. 'In the first place—' she took a deep breath in an attempt to control her feelings—'I do not consider I have a "void in my life". Men are tiresome, interfering, boorish, dictatorial, and—' she paused to place particular emphasis on the final word—'dull.'

He threw back his head and laughed aloud, adding to her ire. 'I believe you have encountered the wrong men, Miss Hyde. Or perhaps it is the lack of encountering *any* men that has caused you to view the members of my sex in such a disastrous manner?' He added quickly, 'Perhaps I am addressing a young miss who has never been out of the schoolroom until this ill-fated journey.'

Was there no end to the man's insults? 'I have been out of the schoolroom for some time, Mr Kingston. I have been presented in London, and I have had more than one offer for my hand, all of which I most emphatically declined!'

He reached under her chin and turned her face to his to study it. The early light of dawn had greyed the sky and it was easy to view each other. 'So you are out of the schoolroom. How old are you, Miss Hyde?'

She saw the twinkle in his grey eyes; it softened the harshness of his features, but it was also there at her expense, and she felt no appreciation for it. She jerked her face away.

'I am almost twenty-one, and no longer will need a guardian. And you, sir, ask highly improper questions!'

The amusement in his voice was unmistakable. 'Such unbending coldness, Miss Hyde, like a diamond encased in glass in a museum—glittering, untouchable, and cold. Ah, but you are not an inanimate diamond; I feel that behind the aloof barrier you present there is a heart. A young woman who is so wilful must have a heart which can be warmed by someone. Who were the suitors who offered for you?'

'I have no intention of discussing that with you!'

The lane dipped and disappeared under a shallow stream. The horse plodded steadily through the water and across to the other side. Jared turned her face towards him again in a quick movement and stared down at her. 'I suspect they were quite young and green. Now do not flash those angry eyes at me, Miss Hyde; you give yourself away when you do.'

'You are the most insulting man I have ever had the misfortune to meet!'

'And there is no one, so far, you care to marry?' he persisted.

She snapped, 'I shall never marry!' Immediately she wished she could retract the words; they would only add to his questions.

'Never?' he repeated; his eyes searched her face. 'Never is a strong word, Miss Hyde.'

'I feel quite strongly on the matter.'

'That is a unique attitude, as a matter of fact, one I never have encountered before in a female. What precipitated this drastic decision?'

She turned and glared at him. 'You think I am not sincere? Well, indeed I am!'

He studied her intently, tilting his head to one side. 'Did you have a cruel father who beat you?'

She raised her chin slightly higher. 'No, I did not. My father had little time for me—I hardly knew him.'

'Something has caused you to feel this way,' he mused aloud.

'I want my freedom,' she answered. 'I find men dictatorial. Now that I will soon be of age, I can do as I please. I do not care to marry and have to answer to someone else just as I did as a child.'

'There are compensations for curtailment of your freedom, Miss Hyde. Do you not long for a man's strong arms, or have you never enjoyed a man's kiss?'

'That is impertinent, sir! I do not care to listen to another question; I would much prefer to walk!' She flung the angry words at him and slid quickly off the slow-moving animal.

She hurried ahead, but he merely caught up and allowed the horse to keep pace beside her. 'Miss Hyde, 'tis a long walk to Louisiana. Come back up here into my arms.'

She raised her chin and walked faster, causing the blue

organdy skirt to swirl against her legs. He laughed and said lightly, 'I apologise, Miss Hyde. I have been a rogue and I will torment you no longer. Now come here.'

'Indeed not!' she replied without looking up.

Suddenly he dropped lightly to the ground and fell into step beside her. Camilla's lips tightened angrily and she stared straight ahead.

They walked in silence beside the narrow stream. Jared asked, 'Shall we stop for a drink? I would welcome one.'

Camilla did not answer, but halted when he did and sat down on a log beside the water while he drank. When he finished he sat on the grass near her and she looked away, viewing the peaceful countryside intently. On the horizon lightning flashed at short intervals, far distant from them and visible only as a steady flickering against the dark rain clouds. The odour of dust was gone, leaving the tantalising smell of rain. She felt his eyes on her and tried to ignore him, but was drawn irresistibly to face him. She met his cool level stare and when he spoke there was no trace of jest in his voice.

'Something must have happened to cause you to feel that way about men.'

She stared at him a moment, noticing the dark bruise on his cheek; it had yellowed and faded, any trace of the thin cut from his mouth was almost gone. A dark stubble of beard had begun to grow on his chin, which caused him to appear more like a pirate than ever.

In a quick sweep she stood. 'Let us be on our way, Mr Kingston. The sooner we reach Louisiana, the sooner I can be on my voyage home.'

He rose and strolled beside her, adding, 'And away from me. Perhaps you need a source of irritation, Miss Hyde, to help you overcome whatever it is that's causing you to hold your emotions in check.'

'I can take care of myself quite well, thank you.'

Undaunted, he continued, 'You need to broaden your acquaintances, instead of limiting it to those damp-fingered dandies who, I suspect, have offered for you.'

'You are every bit as boorish and dull, Mr Kingston,' she flung at him, 'as any "damp-fingered dandies" of my acquaintance!'

'I think,' his voice was filled with mirth, 'I can honestly confess that this is the first time in my life I have ever been told I am dull.'

'And I see you are far too insensitive for it to disturb you in the least!' she replied hotly.

He reached out and caught her arm, gazing down at her with a wicked gleam in his eyes. 'Have you ever really been kissed, Miss Hyde?'

'Don't you dare!' she breathed, and turned to hurry on.

'I thought not,' he declared blithely, 'you are scared to death. You will become an old maid with a frozen heart.'

She walked faster, stamping through the high tufts of grass along the bank of the stream, her cheeks burning in fury. 'You are miserably rude!'

'Spoiled, rich, wilful and cold,' he continued lightly.

'How dare you, sir!' Camilla's temper snapped. She faced him, raising her hand in anger to slap his infuriating face.

He laughed and caught her wrist swiftly. 'Ah, Miss Hyde . . .' He murmured. His arm went round her waist with lightning speed and he pulled her to him. His mouth pressed tightly against hers as he held her close.

Camilla struggled in his arms, but to no avail. Like steel, she was held fast and kissed thoroughly. His lips were warm and demanding on hers, persisting until her struggles ceased and she felt faint. Abruptly he released her and gazed soberly down into her eyes, searching hers with a strange look in his own.

Her breast heaved with emotion and she whirled away from his intense stare. For a moment he walked silently beside her.

'Miss Hyde —' he began, but she interrupted.

'Do not, Mr Kingston, utter another word to me. Some men may find it necessary to hold a girl captive in order to obtain a kiss, but I find it loathsome and disgusting behaviour. It will be easy to forget it this time; just do not attempt such a thing again. It is anything but a pleasant experience.'

He spoke quietly. 'It is time we rode.'

She continued walking but heard the horse stop. Jared mounted, then rode up beside her to hoist her on to the horse's back in front of him. After a few moments his voice sounded low in her ear.

'I do not think you found it loathsome at all, Miss Hyde. I think you are afraid of your own feelings.'

She did not answer and he fell silent. Each rode lost in their own thoughts while the morning sky lightened. The clouds did not break, but remained overcast, promising a muggy day if rain did not fall. Soon they encountered the rough rails of a log fence. A line of cows moved steadily out to pasture, and within minutes they caught sight of a barn, a house, and a farmer working in the field. Jared urged his horse to a faster pace and they soon reached the man.

He informed them they were nearing Corningsburg. When he asked them to stay for a visit Jared declined, thanked him, and headed in the direction given.

The basket of food had been abandoned in their haste to get away in the night; Camilla was growing hungry, but hid her disappointment when Jared refused to stop. With relief she listened as he declared, 'We will halt at Corningsburg if there is an inn, and I shall purchase another horse. Once again, Miss Hyde, it will arouse less curiosity if I introduce you as my wife.'

'I object. I do not care to stay at an inn as your wife.'

'None the less you will do so. It will be vastly safer; there are settlements here where men have not seen a female for over a year. 'Tis best for you.'

She glared at him. 'That, sir, is exactly what I meant about men being dictatorial. Are you that authoritative with your fianceé?'

He smiled slightly and raised one eyebrow. 'Perhaps I would be if I thought her life depended on it.'

Camilla turned away in disgust, then glanced again at him. 'And I assume she is quite beautiful!'

His lips twitched. 'Absolutely ravishing!' He caught her chin in his warm fingers and added, 'And she is not afraid of her own feelings either, Miss Hyde.'

Camilla jerked away angrily. 'I am not afraid of my feelings. I merely do not intend to get caught in a trap like . . .' she bit off her words and turned away, but they were out and it was too late to stop their effect.

He spoke softly. 'Ah . . . there *is* something that happened. Who were you referring to, Miss Hyde?'

She caught her lip worriedly in her teeth, then stated, 'I said more than I intended, Mr Kingston. You are an extremely persistent person, but it is none of your affair and I would prefer to drop the matter.'

He spoke gently, 'Sometimes you will find that if you face up to your problems, they can be overcome.'

She looked into his grey eyes. 'Have you faced up to your own, Mr Kingston? Have you? Why are you a pirate living in a new territory? Where are you from, and what did you leave behind?'

He gazed down at her soberly for a minute, then replied softly, '*Touché*, Miss Hyde. Perhaps I deserved that.'

She nodded with satisfaction and they rode into town in silence. Corningsburg was a thriving small community with a row of small shops along a narrow twisting lane. In the shade of a spreading elm, wagons and coaches indicated the yard of an inn.

The overhanging half-timbered upper-storey sported a large sign with a painting of a brown owl. By the time they had dismounted and entered the arched door, a light rain had begun to fall; the cold drops spattered against Camilla's cheeks.

Jared introduced her as his wife and partially explained their circumstances. Standing beside him, her head barely reaching his shoulder, Camilla became acutely conscious of her dishevelled appearance. The pale blue organdy was mud-spattered and dirty along the hem; her hair was a mass of tangles.

Her first feeling when the door closed giving them privacy in an upstairs room was relief to be out of sight of the curious stares of fellow-travellers below.

Jared glanced around. 'We are fortunate to find a good inn in such a little-travelled area.'

Accustomed to the old, established inns of the English countryside, Camilla considered it to be extremely modest, but other matters were on her mind. She stared at him and protested, 'We cannot stay in this room together!'

He waved a hand at her, as if shooing away a bothersome insect. 'I am leaving, Miss Hyde. I have errands to run which will give you an opportunity both to refresh yourself and to enjoy the benefits of a feather bed. I suggest you waste no time for you will not have long, and it may be many days before such an opportunity comes your way again.'

He turned to leave. Camilla asked hastily, 'How long . . . how long will you be away?'

'Several hours will be necessary.' He closed the door softly behind him and was gone.

Camilla summoned the innkeeper's wife to request bath water. When the woman returned Camilla handed her the blue organdy and asked if she would wash and iron the dress while she slept. She wore only her shift when she climbed on to the high soft bed. With the soft pillow and the steady patter of raindrops against the panes Camilla was asleep within minutes after stretching out under a light cover.

She was wakened by hearing her name called and opened her eyes to stare up at Jared Kingston standing beside the bed. She gasped and pulled the cover over her bare shoulders.

'Sir!' she exclaimed, doubly shocked at the sight of him. Not only was his presence disturbing, but she was amazed at his attire. No longer did she face a rough Colonial dressed in mud-spattered boots and leather breeches; but a handsome gentleman clad in a fresh white shirt, fawn-coloured breeches, gleaming boots and a plain dark coat. Gone was the stubble of beard, and his brown hair shone with cleanliness.

Before she could say a word, he turned towards the door. 'I have hired a stage, Miss Hyde. You will have to forgo the luxury of a bed because I need to be travelling. I have done my best to find something else for you to wear; I am certain that by now you are quite ready for a change.' He reached the door and waved his hand in the direction of the foot of the bed.

Camilla glanced down and saw a dress and pelisse stretched over her feet. 'But where . . .?' she started to inquire, only to be interrupted.

'The stage waits and I am anxious to leave; please come as quickly as possible.' The door closed behind him.

Camilla threw off the cover and stepped down out of the high bed to lift the dress in her hands. It was a delicate rose muslin with a rose silk pelisse. She slipped it over her head hastily and was surprised to find that it fitted fairly well; it was slightly too large in the waist.

She glanced at the door through which Jared had just gone, her thoughts lost in curious wonder over where he had obtained the clothing and how he had known what would fit. She shoved her thoughts aside and continued to get ready. When she lifted the pelisse she noticed another small object on the bed—a hairbrush.

Camilla smiled and rushed to the mirror while pulling the bristles through her tangled tresses. She summoned the innkeeper's wife to fetch the blue organdy dress, then descended to join Jared downstairs with the organdy rolled into a small bundle under her arm.

They rushed outside through the gentle rain to a waiting coach and driver. Jared opened the door for her, then climbed in and sat down facing her. He placed the familiar pistol on the seat in the corner of the coach.

A small basket with a piece of white linen covering its contents rested on the seat, and as soon as they were moving Jared lifted it to his lap. 'I asked the innkeeper to pack a basket of food for us to take—it will be faster this way.' He removed the cloth to reveal thin slices of cold turkey, freshly baked bread still warm from the oven, apples, and a bottle of wine.

Camilla regarded him. 'Thank you for the dress and pelisse. Where did you get them, and how did you find them to fit?'

He raised his head and his glance flicked over her. ' 'Twas not simple; I asked the innkeeper's wife to help find clothes.'

He handed her a square of linen, then a piece of bread and placed turkey on it to pass to her. With a tug the cork came out of the wine bottle; Jared lifted a small mug from the basket and studied it with wry amusement. 'The family crystal.' He poured wine into it and extended it to her with a flourish.

She smiled and shook her head, 'No, thank you.'

He shrugged and stated, 'I did not do so well for myself. I must remove this coat; 'tis too snug to be comfortable.'

Camilla noticed then the pull of the cloth across his broad shoulders. He slipped off the coat, folded it and placed it on the seat beside him. She studied his dark hair while he bent over the basket to slice the bread.

The food tasted delicious and she relaxed against the seat, thoroughly enjoying the repast. 'You have had little sleep in two days' time,' she observed. 'I would think you'd be weary.'

He lowered his mug of wine and gazed at her. 'I am, but 'tis outweighed by my desire to reach my destination.'

'You are a very persistent person.'

'There is a fortune involved in each of those ships. I have no intention of losing them.'

She bit into the tender turkey and fluffy bread while considering his actions. He had hired a stage, had in some way acquired new clothes for each of them and paid the innkeeper for food and room. He obviously did not lack funds, yet he was driving himself to acquire more. Was money that important to him? she wondered. The rain drummed lightly against the coach; the sound of the drops mingled with the noise of the wheels and the horses' hooves.

Jared Kingston finished eating, folded the linen square into the basket beside his empty mug and placed the basket on the floor. Then he turned into the corner of the seat and stretched his long legs out as far as it was possible.

She asked, 'Ready for a nap now?'

'I shall be, shortly.' He studied her a moment, then asked, 'You said you and your uncle were travelling when he took ill—what was your journey?'

Camilla wiped the tips of her fingers with the linen. 'We had been around the world.'

His eyebrows raised. 'Around the world! Indeed, you are a traveller. Isn't that unusual for so young a lady?'

'Yes, but my life is not like that of other young ladies.'

'Ah yes, you said your life had been spent with men, and that you have no intention of marrying.'

She folded the square of linen rapidly. 'That is correct. Please, Mr Kingston, I do not care to spend the afternoon discussing myself.'

He crossed his arms over his chest and gazed intently at her. 'But I find that a fascinating thought, Miss Hyde—distinctly unique in a young lady who is quite pretty.'

'After benefit of bath and hairbrush?' she retorted.

The corners of his mouth twitched. 'Prettier—with their benefit. Why do you not want to marry?'

She leaned down and placed the linen square in the basket, then raised her head to meet his steady gaze. 'Why should I want to? It is of advantage only to the man.'

'Miss Hyde!' He straightened and placed his booted feet squarely on the carriage floor to study her even more intently. 'Such a novel thought! How could it have gotten into your pretty head?'

Her green eyes flashed. 'Look at the O'Neals. She is only a year older than I am, yet she is burdened with work the whole day long, all because of marriage.'

Jared answered easily, 'Her appearance did not give an

indication of much suffering, or misery with her lot.' He cocked his head to one side and regarded her. 'Besides, you felt that way before you met the O'Neals.'

She glanced quickly at him, but did not answer.

'What are you afraid of?' he persisted.

Her temper snapped and she said, 'My elder sister, Jane, had a marriage arranged by our father, and it was most unfortunate.'

'Is she still married?' he asked.

'She is dead,' Camilla told him. 'He was a cruel and treacherous man and caused her death.'

Jared sobered. 'That sounds most unfortunate, but you cannot blame all men for such an event, or expect them all to act in such a manner.' He smiled at her. 'Your father is no longer alive to arrange an unwanted marriage for you. You will never suffer such a fate.'

'Indeed I will not!'

He leaned forward. 'Someday, Miss Hyde, some man will melt your icy heart.'

Camilla shifted and stared out at the rain. 'You are teasing me, Mr Kingston. I would feel far more comfortable if we discussed something besides my most personal feelings.'

She allowed a great deal of time to pass before she glanced again in his direction. To her surprise she discovered he was asleep. She relaxed slightly and studied him. His dark lashes were long against his high cheekbones. He was settled squarely in the corner of the coach with his arms still folded across his chest. Dark curls tumbled over his forehead and when asleep—and no longer a source of irritation—he was quite handsome. What had he done to cause him to live in Louisiana, or had he been born there? Her curiosity was aroused. And what was the ravishing French fianceé like?

Her eyes travelled to the firm mouth, still in repose, and against her will the memory of his kiss returned. She looked away quickly and tried to forget the warm feelings it stirred.

With determination she forced her thoughts to Mrs

Madison and the last few hours at the mansion. Within minutes, drowsiness overtook Camilla and she too slept.

When she awoke it was with a start of surprise in a quick moment of forgetfulness of her circumstances. The interior of the coach was dark and she stared blankly at it, then remembered.

'Awake now, Miss Hyde?' Jared inquired.

She hid a yawn behind her hand. 'Yes, I must have slept the entire afternoon.'

'And part of the evening,' he added cheerfully. 'Are you ready for another slice of cold turkey and what will now be cold bread?' He added, 'The rain has long since stopped.'

She agreed, and to her relief he called to the driver to halt and allowed her to get out to stretch for a time. After they had eaten they climbed inside, and once again resumed their journey.

'We shall stop soon and change horses at an inn. It will give you another few moments to freshen up. We are making excellent time.'

Suddenly, as if in defiance of his words, the coach rocked to a jarring halt. A voice outside bellowed, 'Stand and deliver!'

CHAPTER
FOUR

JARED snatched up the long-barrelled pistol and whispered,
'Highwaymen!'

Camilla stiffened and peered through the window. Out of
the corner of her eye she caught a swift movement as Jared
yanked on his coat and tucked the pistol into his waistband.

'Do be careful,' she cautioned.

Surprisingly, he grinned through the darkness at her. 'I see
I have no fainting miss on my hands.'

The coach door was flung open and a gruff voice ordered,
'Outside with ye, and be quick or your man dies!'

Jared emerged, turned and took Camilla's hand to assist
her down. He moved away from her a few feet until the
highwayman ordered him to halt.

They faced only one robber as they stood in a small clearing
surrounded closely by high shrubs. The ruffian was dressed
in top-boots, a long-tailed black coat, and wore a mask over
his face. A long black beard flowed out beneath the mask,
and he brandished a pistol at them. 'Toss your valuables on
the ground and be quick!'

'I . . . I have none,' Camilla stated.

'Such a lady—and no valuables? Do not lie to me, ma'am!'

Jared tossed a few coins in the dirt and answered calmly,
'She is telling the truth. Her things have already been taken
from her. You are a little late.'

The highwayman regarded the coins, then Jared. 'I shall
see. Ye better not be lying.' He moved cautiously to search
Jared, reaching forward with one hand to feel his pockets.

With a swift movement Jared brought his hand up in a
powerful sweep and sent the pistol flying from the thief's

hand. They locked together for an instant, then a hard blow from Jared felled the robber. Even as he toppled to the ground, Camilla heard a rustle close at hand and whirled to discover the long barrel of a pistol protruding from the parted branches of a nearby shrub. Without thought she screamed a warning and flung herself at the weapon to shove it away.

It discharged and a searing pain burned her arm. Almost at the same moment a hand grasped her and flung her to the ground.

Another shot blasted the still night, causing the horses to jump and whinny nervously. Camilla raised herself in alarm, fearing that Jared Kingston might lie wounded at her feet, but he rushed towards her and knelt beside her, dropping his pistol.

'Are you all right?' he asked.

'Yes—yes, I'm not harmed, but you, sir?'

She could hear the relief in his voice. 'Thanks to you, I am quite all right. You saved my life then.' He pulled her to her feet and Camilla gasped involuntarily at the pain in her arm when she moved.

The driver called, ''Tis dead he is, sir!'

'Are you hurt!' Jared exclaimed.

'No,' she protested. 'I am certain it is a mere scratch. It pained me when you helped me up.'

'Fetch me a lantern, man!' Jared commanded the driver. The man obeyed, bringing a lantern quickly, then holding it high for Jared to view Camilla's arm.

She glanced down to see a dark stain of blood on the silk sleeve of the rose pelisse. 'I'm afraid I have ruined the pelisse,' she stated.

There was a commotion behind them and the first highwayman aroused and ran into the darkness. The driver turned to Jared. 'Should I go after him, sir?'

Jared shook his head. 'Let him go; 'tis not worth the trouble. Do you know how far it is to the next town?'

'I figure about two miles, sir.'

'Thank heavens! Get the body on the coach and let us continue. We must find a doctor.'

'Yes, sir,' the man answered, and hurried to do as instructed. Jared led Camilla to the coach, carrying the lantern with him. She climbed inside, he followed and closed the door. He sat down on the seat beside her.

'Now, we should get the pelisse removed and see how deep the wound is.'

Even though he slid the silk wrap from her shoulders gently, Camilla gasped and closed her eyes as the cloth pulled over the injury. She opened them to gaze down while Jared took his handkerchief and touched her arm lightly. 'You see, I told you I was not hurt. It is nothing.'

She looked up into his grey eyes. The lantern's light flickered over his tanned skin, the flame's orange glow making it appear darker than ever. He declared softly, 'You are very brave.'

Embarrassed, she averted her eyes, wishing he did not have such a habit of watching her intensely. 'I am all right,' she murmured and moved slightly away from him.

'Nonetheless, we shall have a doctor look at it; you have a hard journey ahead of you and it will not do for you to fall ill.'

She raised her head to meet his sombre stare and decided that his concern was probably not for her own welfare, but for any inconvenience she might cause him. He continued to regard her in the same direct manner, then leaned down and removed the bottle of wine from the basket to pour her a drink.

She spoke quickly. 'I do not care for any, sir.'

He straightened. 'Miss Hyde, I cannot imagine a single female I have known at any time in my life to go through what you just did and remain so calm. 'Tis most unnatural.'

She smiled slightly. 'I assure you, sir, that I am fine. I have no use for spirits of any sort.'

He studied her, then replied 'Very well,' and replaced the corked bottle in the basket.

The coach began to move, and soon they achieved a good speed. The lantern was hung on a hook just inside the door and swayed with the continual rocking of the vehicle, causing the shadows to dance inside. Jared remained beside her, shifting to face her. 'Is it uncomfortable to ride?' he inquired.

'No, and I feel no need for a doctor. You can see clearly for yourself that the wound is slight.'

He did not reply, but rode in silence until they reached town. The first stop was for him to get directions to a physician's home where the driver was instructed to wait. They aroused the physician from sleep and followed his shuffling steps to a back parlour. Clad in a long robe which was belted over his ample mid-section, the doctor instructed Camilla to sit on a high seat while he moved about the room lighting oil lamps.

'Encountered highwaymen, eh?' he repeated, after Jared's explanation. 'Times are changing; it used to be quite safe, but there are more people now, and perhaps more to gain from robbery.' He halted to examine Camilla's arm and clucked over her. 'My dear, what a scoundrel—to have harmed a pretty wife.' He peered over his spectacles at her, then looked at Jared who was leaning one shoulder against the wall with his arms folded over his chest. 'I see no red eyes from weeping. You have an exceptional wife, sir.'

'Yes, she is quite exceptional,' Jared replied, looking directly into her eyes.

Camilla's blush did not escape the doctor's notice. His eyes twinkled as he inquired of her, 'You've not been wed long, have you?'

'Not long at all,' she replied.

'I will clean this and place a bandage around it for tonight. 'Tis a minor scratch, and within a day or two you will forget you ever suffered it. Excuse me while I fetch my things.'

He shuffled out of the room, then returned shortly with a pitcher of warm water and a bowl. He moved an oil lamp closer to study what he was doing, then dipped a clean cloth

in the water and wrung it out. He paused and glanced at
Camilla. 'This may hurt a bit.' He turned to regard Jared.
'Perhaps you should hold your wife's hand, sir.'

Jared straightened and crossed to take her hand. He smiled
down at her and held it between both of his own. His flesh
was warm against hers.

'You don't need to . . .' she started to say, then broke off
when the doctor touched the wound.

She clamped her lips together and held her breath for
a moment, looking intently at the back of Jared's hand and
the white linen cuff of his sleeve, contrasting with the tan
of his wrist. Finally the doctor was finished, and he stepped
away.

'There, young lady, you will be good as new. Wish all my
female patients were like you.'

Camilla smiled and rose to her feet while he continued
cheerfully, 'I have a family of fainting females; a rodent
scampers across the floor and they all swoon.'

Jared reached into his pocket and produced a thick
sheaf of bills, withdrawing some and handing them to the
doctor.

'Not that much,' the doctor protested, but Jared insisted
and shoved them into his hand, then placed his arm round
Camilla's waist to lead her outside.

They went next to the mayor's home, and Camilla waited
alone in the carriage while Jared and the driver were gone.
When they returned Jared removed the lantern from inside
the coach before he slid on to the seat beside her. The coach
moved again through the night, gathering speed, and soon
they left the small town behind.

'Miss Hyde, you have had a bad night,' Jared observed. 'I
think a glass of wine would be a help.'

'No thank you,' she demurred.

'Would you care to put your head on my shoulder to sleep?
It might be more comfortable.'

'No, Mr Kingston. I am weary, but I feel it might be more
comfortable for both of us if you would ride across from me.'

He shifted places and Camilla turned to lean against the back of the seat with her good arm. She did not care to admit it, but her injured arm ached abominably, her temples throbbed, she was exhausted and felt much different from the calm she had displayed. She closed her eyes, hoping sleep would come and shut out the pain.

The jolting ride was uncomfortable; she moved first one way, then another, growing cold in spite of the fact that it was a summer night. Finally she fell into a fitful sleep to wake with a small cry from a terrible dream.

Instantly Jared was on the seat beside her, his arms sliding around her. 'Miss Hyde!' he exclaimed. 'You are freezing!' He peeled off his coat to place it gingerly around her shoulders in spite of her protests, then he leaned down to pour a mug of wine. He raised it to her lips and said firmly, 'Drink this.'

Camilla obeyed, placing her cold fingers over his warm ones on the mug. He would not lower it until she had drunk every drop, then he lifted her easily on to his lap. When she opened her mouth to protest he spoke sternly.

'Miss Hyde, say no more.' He pushed her head against his shoulder. 'Shh ... by now you should know you can trust me. To ride in my lap and have a sip of wine will not be your undoing—far less than keeping all your feelings so bottled up. A good bout of tears would do wonders for you, I suspect. When did you last cry?'

Camilla sat against him, the wine curled warmly through her insides. Between his coat spread over her and the warmth of his body, she felt the chill going away. He gently stroked her temples while he talked, smoothing her hair back away from her forehead. Vaguely she listened to his question, only half aware of it, more aware of the steady sound of his heartbeat in her ear and the rumble of his voice deep in his chest.

'Cry? I cannot remember ... it was when Little Robin died,' she murmured, then drifted to sleep.

.   .   .   .   .

Once or twice during the night she roused slightly and felt the comforting warmth of his arms holding her close. It was mid-morning before she came fully awake, blinking against the bright sunshiny day. She sat up swiftly in embarrassment.

'Sir, you should have awakened me!' She moved away from him quickly. He smiled and straightened.

'You needed the rest. I feel far better myself, but now that you are awake we will stop soon.'

They halted within the hour at an inn, changed horses, ate breakfast and Camilla removed the bandage. Only a dark thin cut showed on her arm. When they journeyed on they travelled at a steady clip all during the day. Finally at mid-afternoon Jared informed her, 'Soon we will halt for the night. We shall sleep at an inn.'

She turned away from the window. 'I feel you are doing that only for my welfare, and it is not necessary.' She shifted slightly so that he could see her arm. 'It is healing rapidly and I feel fully rested. We can continue in the coach; there is no need to halt. As a matter of fact, Mr Kingston, I feel as much need to complete this journey as I am certain you do.'

He studied her for a moment, then replied, 'Very well, but will you promise to inform me if you grow weary or feel ill?'

'You have my word,' she assured him.

Later, she reflected on that moment. She had underestimated his drive and endurance. They rode in the jarring coach over poorly kept lanes, night and day, until time ran together in a blur of jostling, cramped confinement. She dreamed of beds and feather mattresses, of roast duck, hot bread and plum pudding. Most of their conversations revolved around impersonal subjects or her own background. Any questions about his past were neatly evaded or answered in such generalities that it was impossible to draw any definite conclusions about his life.

One afternoon as they rocked along a steep winding lane Jared suddenly inquired, 'Who was Little Robin?'

Camilla regarded him in surprise. 'My pony—but however did you know his name?'

He smiled and answered, 'The night of the highwayman; I asked you when you had last cried, remember?'

Camilla recalled then, and remembered also the feel of his strong arms about her. 'I see,' she replied, hastening to change the subject. 'What sort of farming do you do, Mr Kingston?'

'Sugar, for the most part. I have built a home in New Orleans, and will show it to you when we arrive.' He sat facing her with his coat off. He lounged back in the seat and placed one booted foot on her seat, next to her skirt. 'We shall have to separate before we go into New Orleans—I shall think of some means.'

'Separate?' she murmured in surprise.

'Yes, we cannot come riding into town together. That would be the end of your good reputation immediately.'

She shrugged. 'I do not intend to remain in New Orleans, and no one at home would know.'

He gave a small mirthless laugh. 'Miss Hyde, you know little of this country. It is filled with people who travel back and forth just as your own father did, between here and England, as well as on the Continent. It would not surprise me in the least if your solicitor knows your whereabouts before your letter reaches him.'

She frowned slightly. 'I never thought of that. I did meet a few people in Washington I had known at home.'

'You may meet more in New Orleans. It is a busy, growing place, drawing many people. No, if you value your reputation in the least, then we shall have to be cautious about getting you into town.'

She stared at him a moment. He appeared totally relaxed, his long frame seemed to fill the coach. 'I suspect you have already decided what we will do.'

His white teeth flashed in a wide grin. 'Also, Miss Hyde, while you may not fret over your own standing in New Orleans, I do not relish having to make lengthy explanations to my fiancée about the presence of a pretty companion at my side.'

She blushed in embarrassment, having given no thought to him. 'Of course, sir, I am sorry.'

He appeared even more amused. 'She is a high-tempered girl, who grows jealous without much provocation.'

Before she thought, she asked, 'You are marrying someone who will be jealous without reason?' Instantly she longed to retract the words as his gaze fastened intently on her. She never could fathom his thoughts, but felt as though he could see into her very mind.

'You would not be jealous, Miss Hyde? I have had little indication that you find it an easy matter to trust anyone other than yourself.'

She blushed. 'If I loved someone sufficiently to consent to marriage, then I would trust them, sir.'

He locked his fingers behind his head and observed her with amusement. There was no way to escape his keen observation and she regarded him uncomfortably. 'How would you ever love sufficiently to wed, if you did not first trust the fellow?' he asked.

Ignoring his question and praying silently that he would forget it, she inquired, 'Then, how will I arrive in New Orleans without damaging either reputation?'

His eyes danced and she knew he was fully aware that she had not replied to his question. 'I shall get a horse and ride ahead. I will part with you when we near New Orleans; then when I arrive I shall inform Paulette and my friends that I have a cousin coming from Mobile. It will be an easy matter from that point; I will have you on your way home within the month.'

'Mr Kingston, I will be grateful to you for ever,' she replied sincerely, unaware of how she appeared with her eyes shining in eager anticipation. 'To be home again and have my horse! To ride over our fields—sir, I have longed for it all these months. There is a favourite place in the orchard—'tis hidden—I can go there and take my books to read undisturbed. Sometimes to avoid my lessons, I would take my horse and go; no one could discover my hiding place.'

He leaned forward and took her hand in his. 'A childhood nook?' he said softly.

She brought her thoughts back to the present and smiled warmly at him. 'Aye.'

'For a lonely little girl,' he finished. He added gently, 'Sometimes childhood places are not the same when we return to them later. 'Tis difficult to go back.'

She looked at him. His face was inches away; the grey eyes fringed with black lashes were staring deeply into her own. Involuntarily she glanced at his mouth. He leaned forward the remaining inches and pressed her lips lightly in a tender kiss.

For an instant she allowed him to do so, then she moved swiftly away, brought back abruptly to the present. 'Sir! Mr Kingston, please.' She yanked her hand away and slid across the seat away from him. She stared out the window in embarrassment, not wanting to acknowledge the tumultuous beating of her heart.

He sat back on the seat and replied easily, 'That did no harm, Miss Hyde.' There was a moment's pause, then he asked quietly, 'Did it?'

She faced him, her cheeks warm. 'Of course not, but I do not care to be kissed by an engaged man, Mr Kingston.'

Her emotions calmed as the conversation moved to an impersonal level, and remained there as they continued the journey. Two more days and nights passed in the close confines of the coach before they halted at an inn. Camilla gazed at it in a thankfulness she would not admit openly. Visions of a bed danced in her mind, and she alighted from the coach with a quickened step. They had made several such stops, but only long enough to eat, refresh themselves and change horses; she feared it would be the same again. She asked timidly, 'Mr Kingston, how long will we remain here?'

To her vast relief he replied, 'I have made arrangements for you to remain.' Then she realised he had referred only to her. He turned to stride ahead, but she caught up with him. 'You said "you". What about yourself, sir?'

He gazed down at her solemnly. 'I am leaving you, Miss Hyde.'

CHAPTER
FIVE

IF a bolt of lightning had struck at her feet she would not have been more shocked. She stared at him, perplexed. 'But, you said we would part when we neared New Orleans; we are not close in the least.'

He turned and looked down at her with those grey eyes like slate, opaque and unreadable. 'Miss Hyde, I must make better time. I cannot be encumbered with a companion, no matter how charming, and must go on horseback. I shall make arrangements for you to remain here, then I shall send for you.' In a swift movement he caught her hand. 'Do not fear that you will be abandoned. I swear I shall fetch you to New Orleans at the first possible moment. This is one time you will have to trust someone besides yourself.'

Camilla suffered a growing chill with each word he uttered. She stared at him, confounded. 'You cannot desert me in this wilderness! We are in this wild country—if something happened to you, or if you forgot—I would never get out of here! No!'

'Miss Hyde . . .' he began, but she interrupted with a rush of words.

'Sir! I beg you, allow me to come with you. I can ride as well as you. If I slow you down, then you can leave me. At least be fair enough to allow me the opportunity to keep pace with you.' She stared up into his eyes, her heart almost halting in fear of his decision.

He sighed heavily. 'It is against my better judgment, but very well, Miss Hyde. Let me caution you, though, the very first moment you cannot keep my pace you will be left at an inn. I shall not yield on this point twice—nor will I slow to accommodate you. I regret the situation, but my ships have first priority.'

Camilla was too relieved to be miffed at the indication that his ships came before any consideration of her. 'Thank you,' she breathed, closing her eyes. She opened them swiftly. 'I shall not disappoint you!'

'And I hope I do not have to disappoint you. I shall make arrangements for our horses. We will leave here within the hour.' He dropped her hand, turned and left. Camilla stared at his broad, erect back as his long legs rapidly covered the yard of the inn, and sighed in the knowledge that there was to be no rest now. How could the man push himself so hard and not drop in his tracks? She said a quick silent prayer that she would be able to stay up with him for she had far less confidence than she had exhibited to him. She hurried into the inn to attend to what she could before Jared Kingston was ready to depart.

Camilla summoned the innkeeper's wife and made a list of requests, assuming that Jared would be responsible for the financial obligation. When the woman returned with the needed things Camilla accepted them eagerly.

With lightning speed she donned a pair of boy's dark breeches, a white full-sleeved shirt which hung over her hands until she turned back the cuffs, and finally a plain dark coat.

She stared at herself in the mirror with the wry conclusion that Aberdine would faint dead away at the sight of her mistress. Instead of a young lady who had always been immaculately groomed in the latest fashion, was a trim figure in boy's clothing with large green eyes above a smattering of freckles which had come with the continuous exposure to the sun. She brushed her black hair and tied it securely behind her neck, then looked down at the rose muslin and the discarded blue organdy. She suffered a strange reluctance to leave the dresses behind, and smiled to herself at the foolishness of such an urge. In the past she had discarded dresses after one wearing without giving them a thought.

She crossed the room to join Jared, then halted and in a swift movement scooped up the silk pelisse, the muslin, and the organdy, rolling them into a ball and tucking it under her arm.

In a private room downstairs Jared was waiting with his back to the door, staring out the window. Even though she slipped quietly into the room and closed the door without a sound, he turned. A slight annoyance ran through her that he appeared to take no notice of her changed appearance.

'I see you are ready,' he stated, making no comment about the male attire.

'Whenever you are,' she replied.

His eyes went over her in silent appraisal. 'I shall have to get another saddle for you; I thought you would prefer to ride side-saddle.' He started towards the door.

'I felt I could keep pace with you better this way,' she said.

He nodded and glanced at the clothes in her hand. 'I will get rid of those for you.' He reached for them.

Camilla made a small movement away from his proffered hand. 'May I take them with me?' she asked.

He looked into her eyes and his voice sounded amused. 'Whatever for, Miss Hyde?'

She stared up at him in consternation, unable to answer his question. He regarded her with amused eyes and quipped, 'A sentimental reminder of our journey?'

Camilla flushed angrily and thrust them into his hands. 'You can dispose of them however you like, Mr Kingston.'

He caught her hands and held them fast as well as the garments, causing him to move a step closer to her. His amused look vanished as he said, 'I was merely teasing. Do not be angry.'

'I no longer want them,' she stated hotly, acutely aware of his nearness and of his hands over hers. A strange feeling enveloped her, disturbing, and one she did not care to acknowledge. Why, when he looked down into her eyes like that, did it cause the feeling that she could not get her breath? His finger raised her chin, turning her mouth up to his. She

wanted to get away from him, yet she stood rooted to the
floor, unable to move or speak, but only to look into those
damnable grey eyes.

'It was not my intention to make fun of you.'

'Please, Mr Kingston ...' she whispered, unable to say
more. She felt engulfed in his unwavering scrutiny.

He spoke softly. 'You will marry some day, Miss Hyde. No
man will be able to resist those beguiling green eyes.' He
leaned forward and placed his lips lightly on hers.

Camilla felt swept with longing, a realisation as disturbing
as the fact that Jared Kingston was engaged. She pushed
against him, tearing her lips away from his. She shoved the
clothing into his hand. 'I will be ready whenever you are,' she
stammered and fled without looking back at him.

Had she waited she would have seen Jared Kingston frown
after her for a long moment, then give a small shake of his
head and stride to the door, glancing at the rumpled clothing
in his hands.

When the innkeeper summoned her and Camilla joined Jared
in the yard, only two high spots of colour on her cheeks
indicated anything was amiss.

Jared was seated on a large grey horse; a wide-brimmed,
flat-crowned black hat rested on the back of his head.
His thick brown hair was secured at his neck in a simple
tie.

She mounted and followed to catch up and urge her black
horse alongside Jared's. Both animals bore saddlebags which
bulged, and blankets rolled and secured behind the saddles.

For several days they had been in mountains, but Camilla
felt they were moving even higher in altitude. The air grew
cooler until midday when the sun was full on them. They
rode in silence most of the day; she did not care to converse
but remained shaken by the light kiss and his earlier remarks.

Jared left a trail and they began to move across country,
climbing a steep mountain past outcroppings of lichen-
covered granite. Mountain oat grass waved with the wind,

and in the afternoon a low cloud floated between the peaks, threatening a shower.

Camilla's tumultuous thoughts belied the calm exterior of the girl riding quietly between tall spruce. She was in a torment, the only comforting thought was that they had ridden more than three hours and the going was easy; it should not be difficult to keep up with Jared.

She was determined not to be left behind. The mere thought was too terrible to contemplate—but perhaps no worse than something else nagging at her mind. There was no way to shut out the remembrance of his lips on hers earlier that day and the great longing she had felt.

She was too honest with herself not to face up to the fact that she had fallen in love with Jared Kingston. Against all reason or judgment, and in spite of his teasing, she had to admit that she was in love.

She had never been in love before, nor did she want to be. She had sincerely not wanted to marry and never expected to.

Now she was not only in love, but had lost her heart to an experienced, extremely handsome man who, she would guess, had claimed a great many hearts before hers, as well as not loving her in return, and besides being engaged to be married.

She spent a short time trying to convince herself that it was the close proximity they had been thrown into which caused her to feel this way, the long days and nights of travel with only Jared's companionship, the hours of sleeping enfolded in his arms. She had always faced her problems squarely and this was no different, but she suspected strongly that had the circumstances been entirely different she would still be in love with him. From the very first she had felt he was unlike any man she had ever known before.

The only conclusion she could come to was that he must never know how she felt. She could not bear him to laugh at her inexperience. She would be thankful when the ship sailed for England, while at the same time it would be almost unbearably painful to leave him.

Once they reached New Orleans and the fiancée was at his side, Camilla felt the hurt would be too great to remain near, and she would be ready to sail as soon as he could make arrangements.

Without halting, they continued the steady pace until the sun dropped behind the high ridge, leaving purple shadows long across the mountains. Light was gone far more quickly than in the lower hill country. Darkness came, and still Jared continued riding. Camilla suffered the first tug of anxiety that it might be more difficult to keep up with him than she had thought.

Her eyes grew accustomed to the dark and she could follow him easily; her horse stayed only a step behind his. Once he turned and asked, 'Are you all right?'

'Yes,' she replied.

'If not, or if you get cold, tell me,' he instructed, and settled with his back to her once again.

Hunger came first, then weariness from the steady plodding, first up long steep slopes, then down. As the night deepened, cold set in and she grew increasingly uncomfortable.

She rode on, shivering and huddling in the saddle, determined whatever else happened not to complain or ask anything of him. At one point her horse stopped, and she raised her head and saw Jared dismount and walk to her. His hand closed quickly over one of hers, then released it. 'Just as I suspected. You are cold.'

He unlashed the blanket from behind her saddle and handed it to her. 'Put that around you. If it does not take care of the chill, then speak up. You will gain nothing by keeping quiet and catching the ague.'

Camilla did as he instructed, and after a short time became sufficiently comfortable to doze frequently.

The days and nights ran together in a blur, even more than the ride in the carriage had. Now, in retrospect, the jolting coach ride seemed like paradise. She could curl in the corner and sleep when she wished; she had not been exposed to the

elements, and many times they had enjoyed each other's
conversation and company. No longer was there any of that,
just incessant riding and following his tall figure until she felt
she had become part of the horse itself.

One night when she dozed fitfully an unearthly scream
rent the air. Camilla snapped awake with such violence she
almost came unseated. Immediately Jared turned and spoke
through the darkness. 'It's a panther, or some kind of big
cat.'

'Panther?' Such a thought had never occurred to her. She
gazed into the darkness which now seemed filled with
menace.

'Don't worry; it sounded far away. Most likely any animal
will be as frightened of you as you are of him.'

One more loud cry sounded, and Camilla shivered violently. She was thankful Jared could not see her, but she wished
the night were gone. 'Are you afraid?' he asked.

'I do not like them.'

'Do you want to ride with me?'

'No,' she replied, and gazed fearfully around her. Jared
chuckled.

'You prefer the panthers?'

She did not answer, but continued to gaze about her, now
fully awake. From that moment on Camilla never felt at ease
during the night.

When they finally came down out of the mountains, the
weather warmed. She knew there had been whole days and
nights when they had not uttered a word to each other. Food
had been scarce and mealtimes were intermittent.

During the early part of the journey Jared had forced her to
accept his hat, and it remained hers for the rest of the way,
shading her face somewhat from the sun and offering protection from the numerous brief showers.

Soon Jared grew a beard and his appearance changed with
the days. Camilla lost all track of time; she had no idea of
where they were or how many days they had been riding. The
intervals between meals seemed to grow longer, but she was

uncertain if it was her imagination. One afternoon she was suffering more than usual from hunger; they were on low flat land, thick with trees, and in some places the horses waded through water. The air had warmed and the heat combined with her fatigue until she toppled from her horse and lost consciousness.

When she came to, she opened her eyes to look up at Jared. He was holding her in his arms, brushing her hair from her eyes.

With consciousness came the realisation that she had slowed his travel. She clutched his arm tightly. 'Please, I am all right. Do not leave me . . .'

He rose and swung her up easily into his arms. He placed her on his horse, gathered her mount's reins, then mounted his own horse and encircled her with his arms, holding her close in front of him.

She gazed up at him and her head reeled, but she tried to ignore it. 'Please, I can ride . . .'

He interrupted her. 'Miss Hyde, do not say more. I will not leave you behind. Close your eyes and do not worry.' He looked down at her. 'I know you are hungry. I have finally spent all the money I carried with me. We shall have to live off the land now, until we arrive at our destination.'

Camilla closed her eyes in exhaustion, unable to comprehend the full significance of what he had said. She had no idea how long it would be until they would complete the journey. Her head was too fuzzy to be concerned with it. He had promised not to leave her; at the moment that was all that mattered. She closed her eyes, placed her head against his shoulder and fell asleep.

She awoke in darkness, and her first conscious thought was the realisation that she was not on horseback. She stirred slightly and felt an arm tighten about her waist. She realised she lay in Jared's arms, stretched full length on something too hard to be a normal bed. He whispered in the darkness, 'Go back to sleep. We will stop for two hours, then continue—sleep while you can.'

She obeyed, unable to stay awake, placing her head in the crook of his arm. When she next awoke she found him standing beside her. 'It is time to leave,' he murmured, and took her hand to pull her to her feet.

Camilla mounted her own horse and they moved away from a small log structure. She asked and learned they had spent the time in a trading post. He fumbled in his coat pocket, then withdrew a small packet, unwrapped it, and handed her something dark and foreign. She looked up questioningly.

''Tis for you to eat. It is dried beef, and will give you a little more strength.'

Camilla accepted it and bit off a piece of the tough leathery meat to chew on. 'How did you get this?' she asked him.

'I traded some things back there.'

'I feel much better now.' Jared's coat, as well as her own, were gone. 'Did you exchange the coats for this?'

'Aye. You will not be needing it any longer,' he stated, a fact which she soon found to be true. They were on lowlands and the air was warmer. They began to move through thick stands of pines which shut out the light to such an extent that the days were almost as dark as night.

Night became a dreaded torture; Camilla could not see her hand before her face while they were weaving among the trees, and insects, with their stinging bites against her exposed skin, were a painful nuisance.

During one of the better times they came upon a narrow trail cut through tall trees. Jared halted and turned his horse to face her. 'Miss Hyde, there is something I must tell you. We may as well dismount and rest a moment.'

Camilla halted, glad for the stop; it was mid-morning and pleasant. She sat on a log and gazed up at him.

Jared stood nearby, looking down at her. 'I told you I have letters of marque to raid both British and Spanish ships, so to them I am indeed what you said—a pirate.' He added quietly, 'And one with a price on his head. We will be entering Spanish territory soon and when we do I will be subject to arrest.'

'Then why go there at all?' she cried.

He propped his foot on the log beside her and rested his arm across his knee to lean down to talk. 'I have a friend, Boisblanc, who lives in the swamps near the Chipola River; he will journey to Pensacola for me and relay word to a man there.'

'Another pirate!' she exclaimed without thought.

'Another privateer, not against the Spanish or British, who lives in Pensacola. He has ships and will be able to reach mine before they sail from Martinique. That way I can get word to my men about the danger; I do not want them to come into New Orleans as usual, but instead to land a short distance along the coast.'

'Is there any other way you can do that?'

He shook his head and brushed a strand of hair out of her eyes. 'No, not in the amount of time I have.' He reached forward and grasped her hand in his. 'You have been a good traveller, Miss Hyde, enduring far beyond what I would have guessed. I shall get you on a ship bound for England as speedily as possible—I promise.'

He leaned forward and kissed her cheek lightly, then straightened and pulled her to her feet.

Camilla experienced a slight dizziness; hunger was a constant, all-consuming thing now. She could not imagine where Jared Kingston acquired his strength. He assisted her to mount, then climbed on to his own saddle and they resumed the grinding journey.

The land changed the next day to something Camilla had never viewed before. They began to move through swampy marshes with tall cypress which trailed streamers of grey moss in the air.

She acknowledged something to herself that she had avoided for several days; she had reached the limit of her strength and endurance. She gripped the saddle tightly and clung, only half-awake part of the time. She was weak with hunger, bone-weary from the gruelling ride, uncomfortable and exhausted. If it was much farther she could not go on with him.

She ceased to observe their surroundings, she simply followed Jared's footsteps, unaware of land, water, of day or night, until suddenly Jared halted and turned to her. 'Miss Hyde!'

Camilla reeled slightly, then came awake with a jerk. 'Yes? Sorry, I must have dozed.'

He turned and drew alongside her. 'We have arrived!' He rose in the stirrups and leaned forward to sweep her on to his own horse in a violent hug; his voice was vibrant, filled with triumph.

'We have done it! We have made it across this continent in record-breaking speed. Regrettably, no one will know except us. My dear, you have been a marvellous traveller!'

How could he be so jubilant? she wondered. 'Are you not weary, sir?'

He laughed aloud. 'It will come upon me, but right now I am too pleased to be concerned with fatigue.' His smile vanished and he turned her face up to peer into her eyes.

'Miss Hyde, we are going to a friend's cabin. Do not be afraid, for he would never harm me or anyone with me.'

She blinked in curiosity. 'Why do you sound as though you want to warn me of something?'

'Boisblanc is a pirate, and a cut-throat. He would not hesitate to murder for a guinea, but he is loyal to those he likes. He is a wanted man and lives back in a swamp to hide from authorities.'

Camilla gazed up at Jared and wondered again what kind of man he was. A pirate, with a murderous friend—yet, in spite of that, her heart was irrevocably his.

He urged his horse forward; the land disappeared under shallow water which was filled with reeds and cat-tails.

'How do you know where you are going?' she asked.

'I have been here before. Boisblanc keeps a dugout hidden near here. We will take it to reach his cabin.'

She glanced around at the dark waters and tall cypress.
'This is strange country.'

''Tis like home. I have grown familiar with swamps and
bayous.'

Jared tugged the reins and dismounted. 'I hope the dugout
is still here.' He glanced at Camilla. 'Wait and do not dismount until I locate it.'

She needed no urging, but sat gazing at the forbidding
area. Within a moment she heard Jared's exclamation
of satisfaction and looked over her shoulder to see him coming.

'I have found it. We will leave the horses here for the time
being.'

'Will they be safe?'

'Aye, Boisblanc will take them somewhere. He keeps a
horse nearby.' He reached for her hand. 'Come now, and
watch your step.'

Camilla dismounted, watched while he tethered the
horses, then followed in his footsteps. She was thankful for
the boots as her feet sank in soft ooze up to her ankles. 'Are
there snakes here?' she asked.

He laughed. 'Snakes, 'gators, terrapins, all kinds of
animals and birds.' He halted and parted a clump of cat-tails
to slide a long narrow boat out ahead of them. Jared stepped
inside then turned to take her hand.

'Steady, now. This will turn over easily.'

Camilla was so thankful to be up out of the black ooze that
she climbed into the crude craft rapidly. Jared lifted a pole
and pushed in the soft mud. They began to move slowly, then
eased into water which was as dark as the mud. Jared sat
facing her and paddled noiselessly. There was an absolute
stillness in the swamp, broken only by an occasional bird call.

The boat glided between tall cypress, past ferns and creep-
ers and short crooked stumps which twisted up out of the
water. When Camilla remarked about one of these, Jared told
her, 'They are called knees of the cypress. Eventually they
will grow into trees.'

What little sun penetrated the swamp cast linear shadows from the trees, across water which was so opaque as to appear solid. The wraith-like draping of moss added an unearthly greyness in the air. Camilla locked her hands in her lap and spoke in hushed tones to Jared. 'I never have seen any place like this.'

He glanced around. 'Men have disappeared in such places and are never heard of again. The swamp keeps its secrets well.' He gazed over the water. 'Ships which have been pirated have been stripped of their treasures, then sunk in swamps like this.'

She stared at him and could not refrain from asking, 'Have you done that?'

He regarded her solemnly. 'No, but I know men who have.'

She longed to ask him how he came to be a privateer, what had driven him to seek his fortune in such a way, and where he was from, but she held her peace.

A movement in the water caught her eye. The dark nose of a snake sliced through the murky swamp with small waves streaming away from its head. 'There's a snake,' she breathed.

Jared glanced down. 'The swamp is probably filled with moccasins,' he remarked, and continued paddling. The small dugout turned in a wide arc through the trees and a cabin came into view.

Constructed of weatherbeaten dark boards, the cabin rested on stilts, with a high slanting roof which covered a wide porch. Jared rested the paddle across his knees and whistled, one long whistle followed by two quick ones.

The dugout drifted slowly towards the cabin; they waited in total silence which was broken when Camilla asked, 'How do you know this man?'

'From my earlier privateering days,' came an abrupt reply.

Any more questions she might have had ended when the door opened and a man appeared on the porch. Jared waved to the cabin and jumped up on to the porch to clasp the man's hand. They shook hands warmly, then Jared turned and introduced the pirate Boisblanc to Camilla.

Boisblanc was a small, wizened man who looked as if he could not harm a lamb, but after Jared gave her a hand up to the porch and they entered the cabin, a myriad collection of all types and sizes of weapons belied his mild appearance. Along a wall of the one room home were flint-locks, pistols and rifles, a sabre, bullet moulds, a dagger and strange looking weapons with wide blades and long handles.

Opposite a fireplace was a bed constructed of cypress logs, and in the centre of the cabin was a table with a long bench. Two wooden rocking-chairs faced the hearth.

The moment Jared explained that they had been travelling and without a regular meal in days, living on dried beef and occasional game, Boisblanc rose and began to fetch food and drink, bringing shrimp and slices of a cold meat which was foreign to Camilla's taste.

Camilla ate cold cornbread and cold *soup-en-famille* while Jared explained his mission to Boisblanc and asked his aid in going into Pensacola. Boisblanc agreed, and while they finished he pulled on a deerskin jacket, selected a flintlock and told them goodbye with a promise to see to the care of Jared's horses.

Jared opened a bottle of rum and poured it into tall mugs fashioned of leather and studded with pewter. He offered one to Camilla which she sipped hesitantly. 'Feel better now?' he asked.

She nodded. 'I do not know which I desire most, to eat or to sleep.' She took a bite of meat and glanced at him. 'Everything tastes delicious; what is this we're eating?'

He lowered his mug and grinned at her. 'I suspect, Miss Hyde, that is a question you would rather have remain unanswered.'

She swallowed a bite of cornbread and returned his smile. 'I think you are teasing me again, but at the moment I consider it delicious and do not care what it is, except that I am curious.'

''Tis opossum,' he answered with merriment in his eyes.

'I am unfamiliar with that animal; perhaps 'tis best you do not explain further.' She could not control a yawn and covered her mouth with her hand. They both had finished eating, and Camilla rose to clear away the dishes. Jared extinguished the lamps until only a small one burned.

'You sleep in the bed, Miss Hyde.'

'When will your friend return?'

'Not any time soon; he has a fair journey ahead of him.' Jared settled in a rocker and placed his feet on a bench. He leaned back and closed his eyes; and within minutes he was fast asleep.

Camilla removed a quilt from the bed and placed it over Jared. She stared down at him; his dark hair curled thickly over his forehead and against his collar. She longed to kneel and place her lips against his cheek, but she knew she dared not. She studied his features as if committing them to memory, then extinguished the remaining light and crossed the room to stretch out on the bed.

With her ear against the mattress she noticed strange rustling noises when she shifted or moved. It was not a feather bed, but whatever stuffing the mattress held, it felt marvellous after nights of dozing in the saddle or catching an hour's sleep on the ground. Within a minute she was asleep.

When she wakened it was to a cabin full of sunshine, delicious odours and no sign of Jared. She rose and saw a small fire in the hearth with an iron pot hanging above it. To one side, but close enough to be hot, was a coffee-pot. Camilla yawned, stretched, and crossed the room to pour a cup of coffee.

The door opened and Jared entered. His dark hair was plastered in wet ringlets to his head, his chest was bare above buckskins and his shoulders glistened with drops of water. Suddenly she was aware of her own dusty and dishevelled appearance. 'Have you bathed?' she asked in wonder.

He smiled. 'I have taken a swim.'

Camilla stared at him aghast. 'In this swamp?'

He crossed to pour a cup of coffee. 'Boisblanc has built this cabin near a channel of water which is not brackish. 'Tis not bad.'

'It is full of snakes!'

He shrugged. 'I did not encounter any.' His glance raked over her. 'Unless you care to swim, you may have to wait until we reach Mobile for a bath in a tub. Boisblanc has no such luxury here.'

Camilla glanced at a pitcher and bowl on a sturdy chest. 'I shall manage without the swim.'

'Very well.' He placed his empty cup on the table and crossed to the door. 'I shall see you after a while, Miss Hyde, I intend to take the dugout and catch some fish.' He nodded and closed the door behind him.

By the time he returned the sun was below the horizon and darkness was setting in. Camilla had bathed the best she could and felt refreshed after sleep and food. She watched while Jared prepared a dinner of his catch, cleaning the fish, then building another fire for cooking. As he had the night before, Jared slept in the chair, and when she awoke in the morning he was gone again to fish. The time spent together was a peaceful interlude, but she felt a tenseness, and knew Jared was waiting for Boisblanc to return.

One night after they had finished dinner and lighted the lamps a whistle came from outside. Jared crossed the cabin in long strides, and stepped on to the porch with Camilla following to stand close behind him.

''Tis done,' Boisblanc proclaimed.

With startling quickness Jared turned and swung Camilla up in the air, emitting a wild whoop of joy as he did so. 'We have succeeded! We crossed this Continent in record time and I have warned my men of impending danger.' His white teeth flashed. 'Magnificent, Miss Hyde!' He swept her into his arms for a light kiss, quickly releasing her as he turned to watch Boisblanc step on to the porch.

'Boisblanc, we must celebrate!' He placed his arm about her shoulders and propelled her into the cabin ahead of

Boisblanc. When they crossed the threshold his arm dropped away and he moved to stand before the hearth.

Camilla watched Jared, all too aware of the quickening of her heartbeat at his touch. How changed he appeared; his face was wreathed in smiles, his grey eyes were bright with a gaiety she soon found infectious.

Boisblanc produced a dark brown bottle, and while Jared uncorked it with a pop, he rummaged in a corner and returned with a fiddle. Jared fetched tall mugs, poured a hearty amount, and offered one to Camilla.

She shook her head. 'Thank you, but I . . .'

'Do not care for spirits,' he finished for her. He handed the drink to Boisblanc and poured more for himself, then sat down at the table and propped one foot on the bench, resting his arm on his knee. Boisblanc sat at one end of the hearth and began to play softly on the fiddle.

CHAPTER
SIX

SOON Jared and Boisblanc were singing lusty frontier songs with strange lyrics, and clearly as American as anything she had encountered during her stay. Then Boisblanc launched into a French song, a ditty which sounded as if it had originated with sailors. Jared sang along without pause, and she studied him in the soft light; her curiosity was roused once again at his past. He sang in French with a perfect accent. He knew the language well—was it his native tongue?

The lamps' flickering glow softened his features, now relaxed and happy. His grey eyes twinkled; Camilla watched his throat work as he raised the mug high and drank deeply.

Boisblanc also drank and the silence in the cabin was strange after all the hearty singing.

Jared wiped his mouth with the back of his hand and asked Boisblanc, 'Do you know *Yellow Bird*?' Boisblanc shook his head and Jared began to sing.

It was an old English song Camilla had not sung since childhood. She gazed at him. His dark hair was tumbled in disarray across his forehead and with his white shirt, buckskin breeches, and dark beard he looked every bit a pirate.

How did he know the French song, and even more curious, how did he know an obscure English ballad? As quickly as she wondered those things Camilla also recognised once more how deeply in love she had fallen with him.

Would she be able to stand parting with him, leaving for England and knowing his heart belonged to another woman? She remembered when she had quizzed him about his fiancée's appearance, and his amused answer, 'absolutely ravishing'.

Unbidden, the memory stole into her thoughts of the kiss he had given her so long ago when they were still in Virginia. For ever she would remember his mouth upon hers. His grey eyes shifted and he looked into hers.

Camilla looked down at her hands quickly, frightened lest he discern her thoughts in the uncanny manner he had done on several previous occasions.

'Miss Hyde,' he paused in his singing, 'can you not join me? 'Tis an old English song.' Without waiting for an answer he commenced singing again. Boisblanc began to pick up bits of the tune, skipping places then strumming and catching in again.

Camilla smiled in return at Jared and began to sing. Their voices blended and rang out in the small space and soon Camilla was enjoying herself more than she had at any time since she set foot on American soil.

Finally Boisblanc arose and wished them goodnight, then closed the cabin door behind him. Camilla glanced at Jared. 'Where is he going?'

Jared shrugged. 'Most likely to sleep on the porch.'

She looked at the closed door. 'I feel terrible that he leaves his home to us and goes out to sleep with the mosquitoes.'

'He does not want to intrude on our privacy.' Jared finished the contents of the mug in his hand, then smiled at her. 'After all, he is a romantic, sentimental Frenchman at heart.'

Camilla glanced at the weapons displayed on the wall. 'I am not certain your description fits. What is so romantic? He knows I am "Miss Hyde".'

Jared appeared amused. 'He thinks you are my mistress.'

'Mistress!' Her cheeks grew warm. She glanced at the door, then back to Jared. 'I suppose you did not deny it.'

'In my usual ungentlemanly fashion, I did not.'

Camilla could not resist. She laughed, 'I would prefer you inform him of the truth.'

Jared extinguished the lights. 'He would not believe me.'

He looked at her. 'Miss Hyde, we will leave for Mobile early in the morning.'

She crossed and stretched out on the bed as the final light was gone and darkness enveloped them. She had had a long night's rest the last evening, and sleep was slower coming. She lay in the darkness aware of Jared's presence so close at hand. She turned her head to gaze in his direction, but could see little in the dark cabin.

'This is a strange mattress. It makes small noises when I move.'

His voice was sleep-filled. ''Tis filled with moss from the trees.'

She was soon asleep, her last waking thought of black-lashed, grey eyes.

They bade Boisblanc farewell early in the day, claimed their horses and once more were on their journey with a large amount of food packed by Boisblanc for them to carry along.

The journey was leisurely and uneventful with Jared in the best of humours. They reached Mobile and Jared obtained rooms in a hotel. As they climbed the stairs and walked down the hall he informed her, 'I have still claimed you as my wife. You will have to take my word for it, you are much safer this way. At least you will have your own room and be free of my presence.'

She glanced up at him. 'Thank you,' she replied quietly.

He unlocked the door and opened it to her room, then followed her inside. 'I am right next door if you need me.'

He gazed at her soberly. 'Miss Hyde, I have a request, and I hope most fervently that you will comply with my wishes. Please remain in your room. We will not be here long. I shall purchase clothes for you, but we cannot run the risk of you encountering somebody you know.'

'I think that highly unlikely,' she replied.

He shook his head. 'It is far more likely than you can

imagine. This is a busy port and a growing city with men coming and going constantly. There would be no way to explain your presence, and I have no intention of announcing that we have travelled together all this time. I am certain you understand what that would do to your reputation.'

Her cheeks flamed and she turned away. 'You need say no more. I will remain here.'

'Excellent! I knew you would understand. I shall purchase some clothes for you . . .'

She interrupted, 'But I thought you had spent everything.'

'I did,' he answered, 'but we are in Mobile now. I have acquaintances here who will advance me funds; when I reach New Orleans I will return the amount. Now, I shall get clothes; you cannot appear on my doorstep in that attire. No explanations would suffice.' He crossed to the door. 'I shall return shortly and we will dine together tonight.'

The door closed behind him as he left. Camilla surveyed the tidy hotel room. A large four-poster bed was in the centre of the room, close to wide windows which overlooked the front of the hotel. The furnishings were plain, but comfortable. She summoned a maid to ask for a tub to be brought to her room, and at long last had the luxury of a hot bath.

After washing her hair and bathing she had nothing to wear but the same boyish clothing she had travelled in. She had lost sufficient weight from the rigours of the journey for the clothes to hang loosely on her.

Within an hour after she had dressed a knock sounded and Jared appeared loaded with bundles in his arms.

He placed them on the bed and expressed the hope that the purchases would fit, then departed. Camilla rushed to open first one box, then another, and looked with joy at a pale blue sprigged muslin, a green silk riding habit, a pink dimity, and a pale yellow organdy dress. There was also a white nightgown and blue organdy robe. The garments fitted sufficiently well, and she selected the yellow organdy to wear for dinner.

Before she joined Jared she studied her reflection in the

mirror. Gone were the tangles from her hair; it hung in soft curls over her shoulders above the organdy dress which had a high neck and dainty short sleeves. She donned new slippers which Jared had purchased, and tossed the high boots aside gratefully.

When she joined Jared in a private room downstairs the first thing she noticed was that he had acquired new clothes for himself; his elegant handsomeness was etched in her mind as she gazed at his dark blue coat which fastened neatly over an immaculate white-frilled shirt and fawn coloured breeches. His hessians gleamed, no longer mud-spattered from travel.

He turned and his eyes went over her appreciatively. 'You look none the worse from the trek.'

'I feel much better now.'

He waved his hand towards a table set for two. 'We will eat in here. I do not want to take a chance of meeting anyone.'

She crossed to be seated at a table which was set with china and pewter. The room's furnishings were plain; a braided oval rug rested on boards which gleamed with polish. Jared moved from behind her chair to sit facing her.

Camilla asked, 'Did you see any of your acquaintances today?'

'Yes . . .' He was interrupted by a knock on the door and a maid entered bearing a large tray of steaming food. A *bouillabaisse* was placed before them with thick slices of hot bread and cups of black coffee. As soon as the girl departed, Jared continued, 'I have been told that General Jackson is at Fort Bowyer, across the bay from Mobile. I want to call on him tomorrow.'

'Do you have news of the war?'

'Yes, General Jackson has been made commander of Military District Number Seven, which includes Tennessee, Louisiana and the Mississippi Territory. He is to protect the Gulf coast and word has it that the main line of attack by the British will soon be New Orleans.'

Jared sipped his wine, then continued, 'By occupying Fort

Bowyer, which they did shortly before the end of August, they have ensured that the British will not invade through Mobile.'

'How can they be certain?' Camilla asked.

'The British attacked the Fort in September and lost one ship, the *Hermes*; their casualties were one hundred and sixty-two killed. Major William Lawrence, who was in command of the outpost, claimed four Americans dead. Since then there have been no more attacks by the British.' After a moment Jared replaced his spoon in his plate and said, 'Rumour is that Sir William H. Percy has sent dispatches to Lafitte to solicit his help.'

'Who is Lafitte?'

Jared smiled. 'Another of my privateer friends, as well as his brothers, Pierre and Dominic You. Jean has a home on Grande Terre, and he rules like a monarch; Barataria and the people who live in its bayous are under his control. He is concerned with all the smuggling which takes place around New Orleans. He has a blacksmith shop and a shop of assorted merchandise on Royal Street.'

She gazed at him, puzzled about such a manner of living. 'You speak of smuggling as if it were legal.'

Jared shrugged. 'New Orleans has constantly been a closed port, first by one nation, then another, with blockades and high embargoes. Smuggling is a way of life and was for years before the Lafitte brothers appeared. Everyone in New Orleans is affected by it.'

He sipped his wine, then said, 'There are moments when Claiborne, the governor, attempts to curtail the smuggling. The United States has placed an embargo on the importation of slaves in an attempt to end the traffic, but they are still brought in by Jean and auctioned at a *chênière* called The Temple.'

The maid re-entered to bring more dishes of delicious food, platters of boiled crayfish, baked oysters and squash stuffed with crabmeat. Camilla asked, 'What is a *chênière*?'

'An island of white shells in the swamp; The Temple is one

of them, with giant oaks surrounding a platform which is built in the centre for slave auctions.'

'Why do you think the next major area of attack will be New Orleans?'

'That is all I have heard today. The blockade has ruined commerce; the price of sugar has risen to twenty-six dollars per hundred pounds. The privateers, as a matter of fact, are the main American offensive on the seas against the British.'

Camilla recalled the President's burning mansion. 'I hope your home is untouched.'

His grey eyes rested on her. 'It was completed only last year. If Lafitte chooses to aid the British, then New Orleans will be theirs with little fight.'

'Is he that powerful?'

Jared nodded and leaned back in his chair. 'Aye, that powerful, and New Orleans may be quite weak. There are too many different interests. I hope the Seventh Military District has many well-seasoned soldiers; I fear they will be needed desperately.' He smiled at her. 'I forget that you are British.'

She gazed into space beyond him. 'There are moments when I do also,' she murmured. Her glance shifted to meet his.

'Who do you have at home, now that your uncle is dead?' he asked.

'The servants. There are no relatives, except a distant cousin in Scotland.'

Jared had finished dinner, and he turned his chair to one side and stretched his long legs before him. 'Perhaps you would rather I did not discuss your countrymen?'

'I do not mind; I do not understand this war anyway.'

'Many others feel the same. America did not like the British impressment of its seamen, nor the blockade of its shores.'

Jared chatted for over an hour with her, then Camilla rose and excused herself to return to her room and bed. After the large meal she was tired and went to sleep within minutes of touching the pillow.

They had one more meal together in the next three days; otherwise Jared was away to see others and food was sent up to Camilla's room by his instruction. The first day alone Camilla did not mind, because she caught up on her rest, but then time became tedious in the same small room, with nothing to occupy her interest while Jared was continually gone from the hotel.

Since their arrival in Mobile Jared had been preoccupied with war conditions and getting home. The intense personal attention he had given her on their journey was gone; it was as if he barely noticed her, while on the other hand Camilla's feelings had moved in the opposite direction. She was violently aware of him; her heart quickened every time she opened the door to meet him. She guessed that the nearness of his fiancée in New Orleans might have caused the change in his manner.

By the third morning she was bored with her room and anxious for him to appear. Dressed in the sprigged muslin Camilla paced back and forth, then crossed to the window to stare at the people on the street below.

Noontime came and passed and there was no sign of Jared. Camilla moved again to the window and remained for half an hour staring at faces to see if she saw one familiar countenance. Her patience at remaining in her room was at an end. She could not see any terrible threat in the sunshine-filled street below.

Having made up her mind, she hurriedly gathered a handkerchief and her reticule. She stepped into the hall and closed the door quietly, realising she was risking Jared's ire, but it seemed a small matter as she would be back in her room long before she would see him again.

Careful to not wander too far from the hotel, Camilla roamed through shops close at hand, enjoying the sights and relieved to break the monotony of staying alone. The afternoon grew warm and she finally returned to the cool shelter of the hotel lobby. She crossed the dark blue carpet for the stairs when her name was called.

'Camilla! Camilla Hyde!'

She turned quickly in surprise and looked up at a familiar face. In a fluster of confusion she forced a smile and stretched out her hand for her father's long-time American friend, Edward Searles.

He clasped her hand in his large one to kiss it lightly, then gazed down at her. 'Camilla Hyde! What are you doing here, in Mobile of all places?' He glanced around. 'Is your uncle here?'

'No,' she replied.

Her mind raced for some way to get free, and he looked down at her curiously. 'What are you doing here?' he repeated. He waited for an answer, beaming at her. Camilla gazed up into his large features, his expectant brown eyes, and was at a complete loss. She could not summon the words—if only she had remained in her room, as Jared had cautioned!

The silence changed and became uncomfortable. His eyes narrowed a fraction.

'I . . . I thought you were in Washington,' she stammered.

'I intended to be, but we could not get through the blockade so we changed course and came to Mobile. You remember I have a home here.' He frowned slightly. 'Camilla, why are you in Mobile?'

Unaccustomed to subterfuge, she could only stare helplessly at him. A voice spoke quietly behind her. 'She is here because I am.'

Camilla's heart dropped. She knew it was Jared before she turned her head to gaze up at him.

'Jared Kingston!' Edward Searles reached out to shake Jared's hand vigorously.

Jared smiled, but Camilla noticed his mouth was white-lipped and she knew he was furious with her. Before anyone could say more, Jared placed his arm lightly about Camilla's shoulders.

She looked up at Jared, wondering if he had taken complete leave of his senses. There was no way to explain such a gesture of familiarity as his arm about her. Her fear heightened into a paralysing numbness. She had heard her father declare Edward Searles's deadly ability at duelling either with sword or pistol. Jared gazed down at her and said firmly, 'I did not realise you knew my wife, sir.'

The older man's eyes widened in surprise; he looked down at Camilla. 'Wife? You have married Jared Kingston?'

She was speechless; all colour drained from her face and she felt as if she might faint. At her nod Edward Searles grasped Jared's hand and shook it firmly. 'By God, I am delighted! Make her a good husband, Kingston; you could not have a better wife.' His glance shifted to her again. 'Where is your uncle, Camilla?'

She informed him of her uncle's death, talking and answering questions without giving thought to her words. Her mind was on the quiet man at her side. She had become far too familiar with Jared not to realise that he was seething with rage.

The afternoon had grown intolerably hot and she wanted to escape from both men, from the fabrication they had just told, and from Edward Searles's probing questions.

'You must have dinner with me,' he invited, causing Camilla to wonder if there would ever be an end to the disastrous encounter.

Jared replied smoothly, 'Thank you, sir, but we are on our honeymoon and just returning to New Orleans.'

Searles clasped Jared on the shoulder. 'Good heavens, my boy! What a doddering old fool I am. You two will not want to have dinner with me anyway. I will leave you immediately.'

He raised Camilla's hand once more in his own. 'My dear, I am so happy for you, but,' he glanced at Jared with a smile, 'if this young rapscallion ever causes you trouble, come find me. You have neither father nor uncle now, and my home is here—I shall never be far away from New Orleans.'

Camilla murmured an answer, unaware of anything she replied. Finally they were excused from his presence. Jared took her arm and steered her towards the stairs. They mounted the polished steps in complete silence; as they strolled along the hall his pace increased.

She looked up at him. 'I am sorry. I didn't think there would be any harm in leaving my room for a short time. I did not think it possible to actually encounter someone I know!'

Jared did not utter a word, but walked straight to her room and threw open the door for her. He slammed it closed behind her and was gone without one word.

Camilla sat down quickly to still her shaking knees. She had thought she had seen him angry on the journey, but she realised that she had no idea of the depth of fury he was suffering at present.

She hugged her knees, thankful that Jared had left her alone. Perhaps his anger would cool shortly. She ran her fingers across her damp brow. Soon they would be leaving Mobile and Edward Searles would be out of their lives. Or at least, out of hers. She realised that if the two men lived in the same region the possibility existed that they would encounter each other again.

She blinked in dismay at the thought that that must be the cause of Jared's fury, then she shoved the idea out of mind. Jared seemed quite able to manage his life, he would think of something. It was over and done and she wanted to forget the encounter.

She hoped they would leave Mobile soon. Jared had planned to go ahead of her, and perhaps by the time she reached New Orleans his anger would have cooled.

She rose and slowly paced the room, having little else to do. The afternoon grew late and still no sign of Jared. She sat in a chair and waited for the dinner hour to come.

Suddenly the door was flung open and banged against the wall causing Camilla to jump slightly.

'Sir!' she exclaimed, looking up to face Jared. Her shock increased at his appearance. His cravat was gone, the white shirt was open at the throat with the blue coat gone as well. In a quick stab of memory she recalled her first sight of him, when he stood in the doorway to the President's mansion: his eyes held the same deadly fury now that they had then.

'Come here!' he ordered with a steadfast gaze which was slate grey and looked as hard as granite.

She dared not refuse, but rose and crossed to stand before him. Her heart pounded in her ears. In her entire life she had never been the target of such controlled anger. There was no mistaking his feelings, even though he regarded her silently.

His hand closed around her wrist in a grip which caused her to wince. 'Please . . .' She bit off the words as she looked up at his face. He turned and pulled her along beside him, his long stride covering the hall to the stairs rapidly.

Camilla rushed to keep up with him. They descended the stairs; at the bottom he relaxed his hold slightly and slowed his step. They crossed the lobby without a word and stepped outside into the fading light at the end of the day.

A carriage waited. Jared motioned for her to enter, then slid across the seat to face her, and banged the door closed. The driver must have already had instructions, Camilla surmised, for the carriage started without a word from Jared.

In the close confines of the vehicle she was assailed by the strong fumes of alcohol on his breath. She wondered if they had started the journey for New Orleans—it would be against his plans to travel ahead, as well as leaving her things behind.

When he stared at her with blazing anger she raised her chin. 'I demand to know where we are going,' she said with far more firmness than she felt.

He looked into her eyes and it took all the courage she could summon to face him. Each word he spoke was clipped and cold, like the plunge of a knife.

'We are going to a justice of the peace to be wed,' he announced.

CHAPTER
SEVEN

WAVES of shock ran through Camilla. 'Wed?' she cried in disbelief. 'We cannot! There is no cause for that!'

He laughed, but there was no mirth in it. 'No cause if I want to experience a short life.'

'What are you talking about?' Camilla clutched the seat and stared at the man opposite her as the carriage rocked along a rough road.

'Do you know what kind of marksman Searles is?' he snapped.

'I have . . .' she found it difficult to answer, 'I have heard he is quite good . . .'

'The best.' The reply was icy. 'He is the best marksman in this country. He is also my friend. If I *could* beat him it would mean his murder!' His eyes blazed. 'I have no intention of killing a friend over you.'

They rode in silence. Camilla experienced a mounting terror. She had thought she was in love, but the man across from her was a stranger. She understood how he could be a pirate, his eyes blazed, his lean mouth was set with anger. She began to fear for her very life. How little she knew him after all their days together! Her mind reeled from fright; she could not think of a thing to say or do to calm him.

The carriage halted and Jared reached out a booted foot to kick open the door; it banged loudly against the side of the carriage causing her to jump once again.

'I refuse to do this!' she cried.

He slid on to the seat beside her and placed both of his hands on either side of her face. 'You will obey me, Miss Hyde. Get out of the carriage,' he ordered.

She whispered, 'Sir . . . we cannot do this . . .'

He did not answer, but leapt to the ground and pulled her out after him. They faced a small frame house. Camilla moved at his side without thought or feeling. Jared pounded on the door, then when it was opened by a tall, greying man, he made introductions and asked to be wed.

Camilla wanted to turn and run for the carriage, but one look at Jared's face and she dared not move from his side. His hand grasped her wrist tightly while he gave the justice of the peace the necessary information.

The driver of the carriage followed them inside; Camilla guessed the man was obeying instructions given earlier by Jared, for he looked extremely nervous while he waited. The wife of the justice of the peace appeared. Camilla stood at Jared's side and went through the ceremony with a thudding heart and ice-cold hands.

She repeated vows which were words without meaning. What next? she wondered. Would he abandon her, or place her on a ship bound for England as he had promised, or take her home to live with him in New Orleans? The last was unthinkable. Her mind ceased to function as she obeyed whatever was instructed.

At last it was over, and they once again rushed to the carriage—this time as man and wife. Camilla was beyond all rational thought except concern for her own survival. Jared Kingston looked as if he could commit murder without giving it a thought.

Darkness had descended while they were inside the house. Jared gave the driver instructions to return to the hotel, then climbed into the carriage. They rode in silence, with Camilla thankful for the merciful darkness which hid those stormy eyes.

The carriage halted, too soon for the hotel. She gazed out and saw the lights of a tavern. She dared not question his actions, but waited in silence. Within minutes the door opened and the driver thrust a bottle into the carriage to hand to Jared.

'Here, sir,' he mumbled.

Light from the tavern spilled into the open vehicle and Camilla closed her eyes at the sight of Jared's countenance. Would this night ever end? The coach began moving again.

Jared opened the bottle; the cork made a small popping noise which jarred her taut nerves. Camilla longed to get away from him, but there was nowhere to go. She was totally at the mercy of this man, who by law was now her husband.

The ride to the hotel seemed to take a thousand years. She longed for the shelter of her room, and to lock her door against him. Once again they crossed the hotel lobby and climbed the stairs in silence. How long ago it seemed since they had left! Her mind raced as they approached their rooms.

If only he would stop at his room and not come near hers. She decided not to allow him to set foot in it. Jared had consumed almost the entire contents of the bottle in the carriage, which would only add to his unreasonableness. Perhaps by the light of day he would be easier to deal with.

They passed his door; with a sinking heart Camilla saw that he had no intention of returning to his own room, but instead continued at her side for her door. She suddenly rushed ahead, flung herself into her room and slammed the door shut behind her.

With a crash which almost sent her to the floor, Jared kicked it open.

'Sir!' she exclaimed. She backed away from him quickly and turned with shaking fingers to light a taper. He closed the door and turned the key in the lock.

The single candle threw long shadows in the room. Camilla faced him bravely, but before she could say a word he spoke. His words cut through the air like a knife and ended any rational argument or thought she had been ready to utter.

'You little bitch!'

Camilla's eyes widened in shock. He approached her slowly and her heart thudded in her ears. She backed away bumping a chair with her leg. Jared reached out and caught her hair in his hand, then tugged on it to tilt her face up towards his. He growled, 'You have trapped me into marriage quite neatly!'

'Trapped?' She gazed up at him; his grey eyes blazed in anger, the glow of the candle highlighted his prominent cheekbones.

'Ho! So innocent! This is what you've been after since we left Washington!'

Camilla cried, ''Tis not true! I never wanted to wed. I did not force you to this—you did it, not I!'

'Indeed,' he snarled. 'And if I had not, then Edward Searles would have run me through, or called me out and killed me within the month. Either that, or I would have had to kill him.'

'How would he have ever known?' she asked. She reached up to free her hair from his painful grasp and gripped wrists which were as firm as iron rods.

'I see Edward Searles far too often,' Jared replied. The fumes of his breath assailed her.

Camilla stared at him in horror, realising that his anger had carried him beyond rational arguments.

'I told you to remain in this room,' he snapped.

'And I explained I was sorry about leaving.'

'Indeed, Mrs Kingston!' He leaned closer, towering over her. 'Well, you wanted marriage, now you damn' well have it!'

He swept her up into his arms and crossed the few steps to the high four-poster bed. Camilla paled and began to struggle in earnest. 'Mr Kingston! Release me!'

Her fright was overwhelming, but her struggles would have been as successful had she attempted to lift a carriage off the ground. He ignored her straining arms and her hands pushing against his chest and flung her on the bed, then knelt above her.

'Let me go!' she cried, filled with terror. His strong arms held her shoulders pinned to the bed.

'Oh, no! You have flaunted that cold innocence at me for

over a month now, and you have succeeded in gaining a wealthy husband. Perhaps you have acquired more than you bargained for!'

'Please, oh, let me free!' she begged, then her words were silenced as he pulled her roughly into his arms and kissed her with his mouth hot and searing, brutal on hers, demanding and punishing at the same time.

She struggled, pushing against shoulders which were like marble pillars, beating against his chest, but he appeared not even to notice.

His hand went behind her back to unfasten the muslin dress. Camilla caught his wrist to jerk his hand away, but she had no sooner removed it than he was working at the fastenings with the other. He caught her wrists and held them tightly behind her back with one hand, all the time with his mouth on hers, his tongue exploring, demanding.

In a swift movement with his free hand he caught dress and shift in his fist and yanked them to her waist, baring her breasts.

Camilla struggled harder to get free; a cry was strangled in her throat as he continued to kiss her. He lowered her to the bed and lay with her held fast in his arms while he kept her hands securely behind her.

His warm fingers found her breast and caressed her tenderly, waking strange new feelings. For an instant he raised his head and his eyes devoured her warm flesh which glowed, creamy and pink in the soft light.

She looked into his grey eyes and there was no mistaking the smouldering desire; he bent his head, and his thick dark curls were soft against her chin as he kissed her throat, then down across her breasts. His tongue was a flame, exploring and awakening passion.

Camilla's struggles ceased; she lay passive in his arms and allowed him to caress her, unaware of the moment when he released his hard grip on her wrists.

A great burning wash of desire kindled and rose within her. She turned to him with a soft moan, parting her lips willingly and raising her arms without conscious thought to lock them around his head. She ran her hand over the hard muscles of his shoulder and through the thick locks at the back of his neck.

With a low cry of ecstasy she gave herself to him and pressed her body against the length of his in eagerness. His weight came down over her as they locked in a tight embrace.

Dimly the idea nagged that she should resist, then that too was driven out of her thoughts by his long hard body pressed against hers, his hands roving over her body.

His lips touched hers; his probing tongue aroused her to greater heights, while his hand slid lightly along her slender leg, tumbled the sprigged muslin skirt in disarray, then caressed her thigh. His hands moved deftly, first one place, then another, heightening her passion.

Suddenly he raised his head and became perfectly still.

Camilla opened her eyes and gazed up at him. The flickering light threw shadows across his face which was inches away from her own.

His grey eyes gazed into hers intently with the same burning anger he had shown earlier. His voice was like a whiplash. 'You will not trick me in such a manner!'

Camilla gazed up at him and longed for his mouth, for his hands against her flesh. 'Trick?' she murmured in confusion.

His jaw hardened and he straightened to sit beside her. His voice was ice, drained of emotion, stripped of anything except coldness.

'You deny tricking me into this marriage, yet how willing you are now! On this entire journey every time I have touched you, I have been pushed away; but now when I am legally your husband, you fall into my arms, a willing and passionate wife.'

He stood beside the bed and towered over her; his dark curls framed his forehead. 'I shall not be trapped by a lovely body and willing arms. The world is full of such.'

'What are you talking about?' she whispered. She sat up

and drew her dress to her chin to cover her nakedness, blushing at the awareness of his unabashed scrutiny.

His knuckles were white as he clenched his fists at his side. He exploded bitterly, 'You are my lawful wife, but the moment we arrive in New Orleans, I shall start proceedings for an annulment. There will be no consummation of this marriage,' his voice hardened, 'and soon, there will be no marriage!'

Shame, embarrassment and anger at the harsh treatment he had used, caused Camilla to snap, 'Get out of my room!'

With a cutting voice he sneered, 'And where is all that warm passion you displayed a moment ago, good wife? Has it vanished when you see your little scheme will not work?'

Camilla glared at him, hating the very sight of him. 'You are low and despicable! I did none of this deliberately. You are drunk with spirits, sir! Please get out.'

A lock of his thick brown hair fell over his forehead. He gazed at her; thin white lines around his mouth gave away his anger. His voice was husky. 'You are very tempting, my dear, but not so much that I would forfeit a lifetime of freedom.'

He spun on his heel and crossed to the door, unlocked it swiftly, and left. It closed softly behind him and Jared Kingston was gone.

Camilla stared after him, her senses reeling from all that had happened. Then, for the first time since she was a small child, she felt hot tears spill across her cheeks. She twisted and flung herself on to the bed to sob, pulling a pillow over her head to muffle her cries.

Not until the grey light of dawn shone through the windows did she fall into a fitful sleep, to be wakened shortly by sunshine warm across her cheek. She rose and discarded the torn muslin dress, washed, then dressed in the yellow organdy.

A knock at the door caused her to jump. She crossed to open the door and face her husband.

Jared had sobered, the only indication of his condition of the night was his eyes, which had reddened slightly. He extended a portmanteau to her. 'Will you pack your things? We will leave as soon as you are ready.'

She accepted it wordlessly and turned to gather her belongings. After a minute she glanced over her shoulder to see him lounging against the door, waiting for her to finish. She worked in silence, and as soon as her meagre possessions had been folded and packed he crossed the room to take the bag from her hand.

Not a word was exchanged between them as she walked with him downstairs and out to a waiting coach. He gave instructions to the driver, then climbed inside and sat down facing her.

As the coach began to move Camilla stared out the window without really noticing anything. Finally she turned and asked Jared, 'Where are we going?'

'To New Orleans,' he answered. 'I am bringing my new wife home,' he stated in such a derogatory tone that she winced.

'Sir, please . . .' she whispered.

'Yes, Mrs Kingston?' he inquired coldly.

'You said we can get an annulment. May I reside at a hotel in New Orleans until we do?'

His lip curled. 'Oh no, you don't. You will do just as I say. You have caused me sufficient trouble for a lifetime, Mrs Kingston.'

With trembling fingers she asked, 'Then may I inquire what arrangements there will be?'

He stared at her. Camilla raised her chin and looked him in the eye, refusing to be intimidated in spite of the wild beating of her heart. She would have felt as much at ease riding with a tiger from the jungle.

'I will take you home and introduce you as my wife, then we shall quietly start the annulment. The instant we have it concluded, I shall see to it that you sail for England just as I promised.'

She nodded. 'Sir,' Camilla forced herself to continue the conversation, 'your fiancée . . .'

He gave a mirthless laugh. 'Paulette may kill you. Take care, madam, my temper is that of a sheep next to hers.'

'She sounds adorable!' Camilla snapped before she thought, and caught a quick flash of anger from him.

'Her feelings are in the open, and—' his voice was hard—'I trust her.'

Camilla blushed at the insult and averted her face by turning toward the window. After a moment she looked at him again. 'How can you explain this to her?'

He gave her a level stare. 'I shall manage my own affairs, thank you.'

She sucked in her breath quickly and again gazed out of the coach window. The autumn morning had hinted a storm, and the day had not altered. The clouds overhead were thick and dark, threatening rain. The coach travelled through a countryside that was nothing like her homeland.

They neared the Gulf, travelling along the flat, low land with trees which leaned to the north, growing in the direction of the prevailing winds, their growth twisted and worn by the sea air. The coach and four raced along the trail without pausing for rest for hours at a time, and Camilla guessed that there would be little stopping until they reached their destination.

The time finally came when they neared New Orleans. They began to pass giant live oaks with broad trunks and spreading limbs draped in grey moss which trailed from the trees like ghostly fingers. Fog began to roll in, drifting in opaque paleness to blur sharp outlines.

Camilla felt trapped in an unreal world. The coach rocked, the creaking wheels and thud of the horses' hooves were the only sharp touch of reality in a world which floated and shifted like clouds with an eerie thickening of the air which could hide almost anything. Inside the coach rode a storm pirate—her husband; a fact which was as unreal as the hidden terrain behind the drifting fog.

Suddenly his hand closed over her wrist in an iron grip and she raised her eyes to meet his, only inches away.

'No one,' he spoke with a slow emphasis which could not be mistaken, 'no one—and this time you will obey me—must know about my ships, where we have been, or what we have done. We married in Washington, in July. No one, except my attorney, will know differently. Until those ships are unloaded, I do not want any mention of my activities. Governor Claiborne would be only too happy to investigate the matter.'

His grip tightened; his eyes were close enough that she could see tiny gold flecks near the pupils. 'Do you understand clearly, Mrs Kingston?' he asked.

She returned his gaze. 'You are hurting me. Take your hand off my wrist,' she ordered, then stated, 'Yes, I do understand.'

They stared at each other, then he straightened and sat back against the seat, looking at her insolently.

Camilla quietly returned the look, not willing to allow him to browbeat her further. He spoke softly. 'You would have made an excellent poker player, Mrs Kingston.'

'I would appreciate it, if you did not refer to me as "Mrs Kingston" any more than necessary.'

He cocked an eyebrow. 'And how should I address you—as Camilla?'

She felt her cheeks grow warm. 'No, but please do not do so unless it is necessary. When we are alone I would prefer "Miss Hyde".'

'But you no longer are Miss Hyde; also I might slip when we are with others. Mrs Kingston you are, and Mrs Kingston you will remain until the annulment.'

'How long will that take?'

'It depends partly on how much I will pay, I would guess.'

She flushed again. 'I shall write to my solicitor. At least I need not rely on your funds if I can contact him.'

He regarded her thoughtfully. 'Do you actually have any funds of your own?'

She glanced his way, feeling her own anger increase. 'Sufficient, sir!' she snapped.

She bit off her words as he turned towards the window. He gazed outside a moment, then glanced again at her. 'You have just entered the grounds of my home, madam.' His eyes narrowed and he stated flatly. 'It is not yours now, and it never will be!'

She caught her breath quickly at his hateful words, then flashed at him, 'Take care, sir, that someone does not place a bullet through your black heart and make me your widow!'

With satisfaction she saw that the remark hit home. His visage darkened and he averted his head.

She peered out the window in curiosity. Fog still swirled hiding any view except the ghostly shadows of big trees along the lane. She expected them to stop at any moment, but as time stretched out and they continued to roll at a fast pace she looked at Jared in surprise.

'Are we still on your land?' she asked, wishing immediately that she had not addressed him.

He merely nodded and she turned once again to the window.

How much land did the man own? A pirate with a volatile temper, capable of hardness and cruelty, yet—she could remember clearly his tenderness with her on the journey, the many times he had held her all through the night, the gentleness when she was hurt by the highwayman, the care when she could no longer keep pace with him. What was his past? The remembrance of his scalding kisses came, and she changed her thoughts abruptly.

The ride continued, and with each additional minute her curiosity about his home grew. Finally the carriage slowed and halted. They looked at each other. He said coldly, 'I am home—this is Belle Havre.' He climbed out and did not wait for her, but went striding towards the house.

Camilla gathered her skirts close and stepped down. Jared had stopped a few feet away. He stood and waited; the mist swirled in a soft greyness surrounding his tall figure.

She paused momentarily to view the house, surprised at its beauty. The main house was stuccoed and painted a mild lemon yellow, with wings built of solid brick. The rounded columns of the lower main floor were of plastered brick, with the colonettes in the gallery of carved cypress under a gently sloping roof. Arched windows and doors with delicate fan transoms graced the structure, which was surrounded by thick green vegetation. It was beautiful and not at all what she had expected. She realised he was waiting and moved forward, attempting to hide her trepidation.

He fell into step beside her and they entered the immense central hall which ran the length of the house. All question that she was dealing with a rustic Colonial who had never been far from home was eliminated at once.

The furniture was Louis XVI and Empire, with Sèvres and Dresden vases, inlaid tables, oil paintings and elaborate gilt mirrors. Upon their entrance a butler greeted Jared warmly; other servants came forward to welcome him home, and Jared presented Camilla as his wife.

He introduced her to the faces turned expectantly in her direction. Standing a few feet away instead of beside her, and it was quite obvious that it was not a loving newly-wed couple standing before them. A Negro woman appeared from a doorway down the hall and greeted him respectfully. Jared turned towards her.

'Selena, this is my wife. Will you ready the white bedroom in the west wing and see to her needs, please?'

She bobbed her head, answering, 'Yessir.'

Jared faced Camilla. 'Ask Selena for anything you want.' He regarded her coolly. 'And now if you will excuse me—' With a nod he turned on his heel and passed her to go outside once again, his boots clicking against the polished boards of the hall floor. Camilla faced the maid in helplessness, suddenly hating Jared Kingston for his insolent manner.

The maid nodded. 'This way, ma'am.'

Camilla followed the large woman up the stairs to the second floor, then down a hall to a bedroom which was decorated with white eyelet curtains and a white organdy spread on a high four-poster mahogany bed.

Camilla requested a tub, wanting nothing so much as to be able to wash away the day's events along with the dust and grime she had encountered along the way.

The maid left on her errand, and Camilla crossed to the window to view the drive below. In front of the house Jared waited while a groom led a magnificent black stallion to him. He mounted, turned the horse and rode down the lane, urging the animal to a canter. Where, she wondered, was he off to in such haste?

When Selena returned she fetched the small portmanteau, then opened the door while two young maids carried in a large brass tub between them. They hurried back and forth, filling it with kettles of steaming water, then left Selena to help Camilla.

After bathing, then washing and brushing her hair dry, Camilla dressed in the pink dimity. She asked, 'Are you a slave, Selena?'

'No, ma'am,' the servant replied. 'Mr Kingston won't have no slaves; not many know that, though. He say no person should belong to another 'less they want to. We're all free.'

Camilla gazed at her thoughtfully. 'Is that unusual around here?'

'Deed. There's lots of freedmen in New Orleans, but it's still unusual. Mr Kingston has bought enough men and set them free, that if any man was to harm him, fifty men would rise up and slit his throat.'

'Do you know Miss Fourier, whom he was to marry?'

'Yes, ma'am.' There was a silence, then Selena added, 'We're right glad to have you, ma'am. High time Mr Kingston married, we need a family in this house.'

Camilla's cheeks grew warm; she gazed into the kindly eyes and suddenly longed to pour out the whole terrible tale, but she knew she dared not. She turned away and moved to slip into her shoes.

'You want anything, let me know,' Selena stated, then bustled from the room and soon the maids appeared to empty the bath-water.

Selena finally announced dinner and led Camilla to the dining-room where she was served and ate alone. After dinner she roamed through the lower floor of the house, then sat at a writing-desk in the library to pen a letter to her solicitor, wondering if it could possibly get through with the war in full swing.

She found a book to read, then with book and letter in hand, returned to her own room. Selena had lighted lamps, and turned down the bed.

Camilla changed to the white nightgown and climbed into bed to read, but found it difficult to keep her mind on the book until finally she laid it across her lap and gazed at the darkened window in a wonder as to how such a strange fate had befallen her.

Hoofbeats sounded, and soon someone rode near to the house, then past it, and the night's silence closed in once again.

Booted feet sounded against the hall floor, then without warning the door flew open and Jared entered the room.

He was still dressed in the same white shirt and fawn-coloured breeches of the day. His hessians were no longer shiny, but dusty. His hair curled in unruly disarray around his head, adding to his roguish appearance. Camilla drew the quilt up to her chin nervously, flushing as his bold eyes swept over her as if there were no covers or gown.

'I have informed Paulette of the truth of the situation. She was not overwhelmed with joy, but she does understand. I have also informed her father.'

He approached the bed and his eyes glittered in anger. His step was steady, but when he neared the bed Camilla realised he had been drinking, and she clutched the covers tightly.

He looked down at her. 'Madam, you have put me through hell tonight.'

Camilla took a deep breath. 'I am sorry, I had no intention to do so. I feel you have brought some of this upon yourself.'

His eyebrows raised and he replied, 'What is done, is done.' His eyes ran slowly and deliberately from her head to her toes. He took a step closer and Camilla snapped, 'Do not come near me!'

His teeth flashed in a malicious grin. 'Never fear; as long as getting the annulment depends upon my having left you untouched, no amount of temptation on your part could prevail on me to do otherwise. I merely stepped closer to talk to you.'

'Very well.' She waited warily.

'The first thing in the morning I shall see my lawyer. I expect he will have to talk with you too.'

Camilla remembered her letter then. 'Sir, I have written a letter to my solicitor. Can you send it for me?'

He nodded. 'I do not think there is any hope of it getting far.'

There was no choice but to get up and get it. Aware of his eyes upon her, Camilla sat up, slid out from under the covers and climbed out of bed. She crossed the room to retrieve the cream-coloured note, then handed it to him.

His eyes bored into her. 'Let us pray, for both our sakes, that an annulment does not take long.' He turned away for the door, then stopped to look at her once again. 'The British Navy is gathering. They have blockaded the port, and they are readying to attack New Orleans. This time, if the British come, you may remain behind without interference from me.'

She turned away quickly, afraid that she would be unable to hide the hurt his sharp words caused her. She looked down at her hands, listening for him to go and feeling hot tears come to her eyes. Within seconds the door closed with a click.

Camilla leaned forward a few inches, placed her head against the cool frame of the window and let the tears spill unheeded over her hands.

.   .   .   .   .

With the resilience of youth, the hurts of the night were not quite so painful when she opened her eyes to the bright sunshine-filled day. Selena appeared and laid out her things, including the yellow organdy dress.

Camilla breakfasted alone, then moved through the house, gazing out the windows at the lawn. Selena informed her that behind the house were forty servants' cabins, stables, hen-houses, a hospital, a smithy, meat-storage and ice houses, a small church, a store, the sugar mill and a grinding mill, and a corn barn, as well as a summerhouse and an outside kitchen.

Camilla had just returned to her room when Martin, the butler, informed her that the master and a guest waited downstairs for her. She followed him down the wide stairs, then entered the drawing room as the servant stood to one side and closed the door behind her.

Jared faced the window, the morning sun highlighting his dark hair and revealing the flawless fit of his dark blue coat across his shoulders. Next to him stood a tall slender man with yellow hair tied at the nape of his neck. Both turned at the sound of the door opening, and Jared spoke. 'Good morning, do come in, Mrs Kingston.'

He looked at the man beside him. 'This, Etienne, is the wife I want to be free of.'

CHAPTER
EIGHT

'CAMILLA, this is my lawyer, Etienne LeGuern.'

Etienne crossed the drawing-room to take Camilla's hand and kiss it lightly. He raised his head and his light blue eyes fastened on her with interest.

Jared strolled to the door. 'I shall leave you to discuss the necessary steps with her, Etienne. If you want me, Martin can summon me.'

He closed the door and she faced Etienne LeGuern. He motioned towards a chair. 'Won't you sit down?' he asked. After she was seated he sank down in a wing chair facing her. 'This should not take long, Mrs Kingston.'

She gazed into his friendly countenance with relief after all the days with the stormy Jared. 'The sooner we can be finished the more relieved I shall be. I do not know how much he explained to you, but my home is in England, and I long to return there.'

'Whereabouts in England?' Etienne asked easily. Camilla replied, and soon found herself answering his questions with the first ease she had known in days. She enjoyed his company; it was a pleasant change to find a man attentive and courteous, chatting idly about nothing of importance, without the probing intensity she always experienced with Jared.

When Etienne rose to leave he took her hand and asked if she would ride with him in the morning. Camilla flushed. 'I would like to, sir, but it would be out of place since I am a married woman—even if it is a mere legal technicality.'

He smiled, not bothered in the least. 'I shall ask Jared if we can ride here. There is no reason not to, then no one will know. Now you cannot refuse.'

Nor did she want to. 'I would be delighted.'

'Excellent.' He bent over her hand, then raised his head and remarked, 'Until tomorrow.'

Within a short time of Etienne's departure Jared entered the room and closed the door. He leaned against it with his hands behind him, looking amused. His voice was touched with sarcasm as he drawled, 'You have conquered Etienne's heart, I do believe. He wants to ride with you in the morning.'

She felt the colour heighten in her cheeks. 'Yes, he said he would speak with you.'

Jared moved across the room to stand near the end of the long row of windows, facing her. 'I told him it would be quite all right with me. There is no reason for me to object, so long as we do not cause more scandal than we shall with the marriage and annulment. Etienne will be discreet.' He studied her. 'You will not be interested in Etienne long, I'll wager. You will soon be bored with him.'

'And how would you know what I find interesting?' She experienced irritation that he should concern himself with something that was none of his affair.

He smiled and moved from the door to stroll leisurely to stand beside one of the windows. 'Etienne is a gentle soul; he is a good man, but far too quiet and peaceful for you, Mrs Kingston.'

She raised her head defiantly. 'Are you suggesting, sir, that I fare better with temperamental men of your own cut?'

Instead of the sharp answer she expected, he said amiably, 'Once again, *touché*, Mrs Kingston.'

She asked, 'Do you think my letter will reach England?'

'The one you gave me last night?' At her nod, he replied, 'I do not know. The British Navy is concentrating forces in Negril Bay on the west coast of Jamaica.' He turned to look out the window. 'I suspect the English know what rich booty lies in New Orleans warehouses which are filled with cotton, sugar, Kentucky whisky and the like, all worth millions.'

'Then you think they will invade New Orleans.'

He turned his attention from the window to her. 'Yes, because they have much to gain,' his voice hardened, 'and they may be able to take it without much opposition.'

She frowned at him. 'Surely New Orleans would not be handed over without opposition?'

Jared locked his hands behind his back and rocked on his heels. 'If they attacked tomorrow they could come right in and assume control. There is only a small Louisiana Militia. General Jackson has not arrived, and the people of New Orleans are accustomed to such changes of possession.' He shook his head grimly. 'At the moment it looks rather bleak to hope for any effective resistance.'

He looked into her eyes. 'Perhaps that is welcome news to you.'

She met his gaze without wavering and replied quietly, 'I would not want to see your home burned. Belle Havre is truly beautiful.'

'Thank you,' he nodded slightly at the compliment. 'I shall have a horse ready for your ride in the morning.'

'Thank you,' she replied, still observing his grey eyes. The air was electric with tension between them, then Camilla looked away and with a murmured excuse left the room.

Her emotions had calmed considerably by the time appointed for the ride. The morning air was cool and refreshing, promising a lovely day, and her spirits rose even more when she greeted Etienne and saw the approval in his eyes of her green silk riding-habit.

A stable boy held the reins while Camilla mounted a beautiful bay mare, and then she urged her horse forward to ride beside Etienne.

They rode in silence for a few moments while Camilla viewed the spreading oaks and watched small birds flutter and light on wide branches. 'One would never know there was anything amiss in our world,' she said slowly.

'Yes, everything here at Belle Havre is beautiful. I pray none of us lose our homes to the British.' As soon as he had uttered the sentence flushed. 'I beg your forgiveness,' he said quickly, 'I could not possibly consider you an enemy.'

Camilla smiled at him and reached across the short distance to pat his hand. 'Please do not concern yourself, I understand fully. You are not my enemy either, sir.'

'You must address me as Etienne. I do insist,' he stated pleasantly.

'Very well,' Camilla replied.

'There are many countries represented in this area.' He waved his hand. 'You are not the only British subject to reside in New Orleans, not in the least. We have a large settlement of Germans. They came nearly one hundred years ago and settled on both banks of the River. There are the Creoles, descendants of the Spanish and the French—always you have the Spanish and the French.' He smiled. 'Even the German names have been changed to the French spelling over the years. Then there are the Baratarians, who lived throughout the whole area west of Grande Terre and Grand Isle, Chênière Caminada, all along there. There are Portuguese—we have everything.' His voice sobered. 'But I fear the British Navy. I have heard there are more than seventy vessels off the coast of Jamaica.'

'Seventy!' Camilla exclaimed, and recalled her conversation the day before with Jared on the same subject. 'Surely they will not be directed to New Orleans?'

'I fear that may be the outcome,' Etienne replied. 'If they take New Orleans, they could move north up the Mississippi to meet their northern troops. Over ten thousand soldiers are in Canada.'

He looked down at her. 'Here now, such a gloomy topic! No more of this on such a beautiful morning with so delightful a companion at my side. Tell me about your home. Do you have brothers and sisters?'

Camilla related her history while enjoying the pleasant ride. At one point they rode a short way in silence, then Camilla asked, 'How difficult will it be to get this annulment?'

He shook his head. 'Quite simple, I think. You were not married in the church. It will not be difficult and I foresee no complications at all.' He regarded her soberly. 'Do you actually want an annulment?'

Camilla looked down at her hands. 'Oh yes, indeed,' she replied. 'He has been so cruel . . .' She stopped, realising too late how much she had revealed.

His blue eyes remained fixed on her. 'I have known Jared a long time and quite well. He is a good man, in spite of the way he has treated you.'

She glanced quickly at him and saw the curiosity in his eyes. He continued, 'Jared has been hurt, and the more I talk with you, the less I can understand the tale he related to me. Would you mind, Mrs Kingston, explaining the circumstances of your marriage?'

She recalled that moment in the carriage when Jared had gripped her wrist and informed her that no one was to know about his ships, or that they had not been married since July. She suddenly was loath to declare a falsity to the pleasant stranger seated beside her. She shook her head. 'I am not free to—I do not know how much Mr Kingston would want me to say.'

Etienne's brows flew together. 'Good heavens, Jared does not beat you, does he?'

She flushed. 'Oh, no! I merely promised not to say much to anyone.'

Etienne reached over and patted her hand lightly. 'Mrs Kingston . . .'

She interrupted him. 'I cannot bear to be called by that name any more than is necessary. Please just say Camilla.'

He smiled and spoke in a gentle tone. 'Camilla—how lovely. Camilla, Jared and I are extremely close friends. He is a good man, as I said. I would trust him with my life. I would never deceive him.' His voice deepened at the last, and she suspected that was what he felt she had done to her husband.

'He told me about rescuing you from the man at the President's mansion, about the long journey you made in order for him to reach his ships. He is like my brother—we are very close.'

She sighed with relief. 'I see. He warned me not to tell anyone about his ships, and to say that we were married in July.'

'I know. That is what I will say in public also.'

Camilla studied the man beside her and wondered what bond held these two opposite temperaments in such a strong friendship. She related what had happened exactly as it had, omitting the hours after the wedding ceremony.

He asked, 'You did not know that you would encounter Edward Searles?'

'Goodness, no! Had I had any idea I never would have left my room.'

The horses halted at a small stream and lowered their heads to drink. Etienne continued the conversation, asking, 'I understood that you already knew Mr Searles.'

'I did. He and my father were good friends.'

'Did you know his home was in Mobile?'

'Yes, but I did not recall or give it a thought. I am in a foreign country, we had come across the continent, and I gave no thought to an old family friend. He was my father's friend, and I had not seen him for over four years.'

'Then you did not search him out, or wait deliberately downstairs to find someone you knew?'

'No!' She turned her head away.

'Jared feels you did, that you have done this solely to trap him into marriage.'

She smoothed the long rough hairs of the horse's mane against the satiny hide. 'I know, he has made that quite clear.'

Etienne spoke softly. 'Jared is an immensely wealthy man, perhaps one of the most affluent in this territory where there are many wealthy men.'

She raised her head quickly and looked at him. 'Did he tell you I did this for his wealth?'

'No. I feel he thinks so, though, without asking him. You have no relatives, no one to return home to. A wealthy husband and fine home might be quite welcome in the circumstances.'

Camilla experienced a rise of anger. 'Sir, my father had several companies; he owned farms and land both here and at home, and he invented several highly profitable things. He was a wealthy man in his own right, as well as was my uncle. I am their sole heir. I do not need Jared Kingston's wealth in the least.'

'Does Jared know this?'

'I have never told him in so many words—not that plainly.' She did not add that the reason for her reluctance to speak plainly was because whenever the subject had come up Jared always goaded her into losing her temper, and she did not care to be on the defensive.

Etienne studied her a moment and stated quietly, 'I feel you have told me the truth, Camilla.'

She looked at him in surprise. 'I have. Indeed, sir, why would I not? Mr Kingston could have inquired of Edward Searles about my background.'

Etienne laughed softly. 'If I know Jared's high temper, he was not thinking of such a thing at the time. Camilla . . .' He paused and she faced him. 'I am sorry if I intruded, or said anything unkind.'

She smiled. 'I am growing accustomed to far more unkind things.'

His eyes narrowed a fraction. 'That is not much like Jared.'

Camilla urged her horse forward across the stream. 'It is too pretty a morning to spend discussing Mr Kingston . . .'

They continued the ride and the time passed rapidly; Camilla was sincerely regretful when they again came in sight of the stables. She accepted without hesitation Etienne's offer to ride again the next morning.

The late November days passed in a blur of waiting with Camilla seeing little of Jared and spending more and more time in the company of Etienne. Men came and went at Belle Havre at all hours of the day and night, and Camilla guessed

that their visits concerned the growing danger of invasion by
the British.

One warm afternoon she was in the parlour with Selena,
going over lists for purchases at the market in New Orleans
when they were interrupted by the appearance of Martin and
a groom.

The butler paused in the doorway to say, ''Scuse me, Mrs
Kingston, may I speak with Selena?'

'Certainly,' Camilla nodded.

The groom, standing behind Martin merely nodded while
the butler looked at Selena and stated, 'Selena, could you
come? The doctor left this morning. That prize mare Mr
Kingston had bred at Nashville is foaling and something is
wrong.'

Selena frowned at him. 'I don't know nothing about
birthin' horses. Where's Hallie or Lurinda?'

'The doctor took Hallie with him, and Lurinda got a baby
coming and she won't leave the cabin. Selena, you know how
Mr Kingston feels about that mare. You gotta come. George
is gone into town; there's no one here!' Martin's tone was
desperate.

'I don't know nothing about horses!' Selena repeated.
'There must be someone at the stables.'

'I tell you, Selena, they're all gone.'

'Please, Selena . . .' the groom added his plea.

Camilla rose and said, 'I will come with you. Perhaps I can
help, I grew up around horses.'

All three servants turned rounded eyes on her, then Martin
spoke quickly. 'This way, Mrs Kingston.' He looked down at
the groom and instructed him, 'You show her.'

Camilla hurried after the slender groom to a stall in the
horse-barn, and knelt in the hay beside the labouring animal.
The minutes passed without heed. Her pink dimity skirt
became littered with hay; it was hot in the stable and perspi-
ration poured from her face, but at long last the young animal
was delivered, a delicate little creature with large brown eyes
and thin legs.

Camilla arose, acknowledging the praise from the congregated servants. Dishevelled and exhausted, she paused at the pump to wash her hands and arms. The ordeal had been more than she cared to admit, and she felt as weak and as trembly as the new foal looked. She pressed her wet fingers against the folds of her skirt and headed for the house and the cool sanctuary of her room.

She rounded a corner of the house to enter from the east, and stopped short. A woman stood on tiptoe, her back to Camilla, kissing Jared. His hands were on her waist, his eyes open. He stepped away from her, and Camilla knew there was no escape from an encounter.

'Good afternoon,' he murmured. His voice was quiet, but his eyes raked over her unkempt appearance.

Camilla became acutely aware of the hair straggling unpinned to fall around her face, her dusty dress and dirt-smudged arms. ''Afternoon,' she replied mechanically. The girl turned and Camilla looked into a pair of exquisite blue eyes with long black lashes.

The girl's white organdy dress was as flawless as the dark skin which it revealed, every chestnut hair was combed into place in high curls framing a dainty heart-shaped face. Curiosity and amusement were unmistakable in the clear blue eyes. A dainty hand raised an ivory fan, but not quickly enough to hide her laughter.

'I see you brought a new housekeeper home with you as well,' she said in a voice which was high-pitched, like a child's, belying her age. 'Have you kept her locked in the stables, Jared?'

Camilla flushed. Jared spoke softly, making unnecessary introductions. Camilla had known from the first instant that she was facing Paulette Fourier.

'Your wife! I am sorry, Mrs Kingston.' The words indicated no such thing, they were uttered blithely with a particular emphasis on the *Mrs* 'My dear, I can recommend an excellent dressmaker and hairdresser, unless of course, you'll not be here long enough to use their services.' With one more sweeping, cursory glance at Camilla, Paulette turned to face Jared and laid her hand on his arm. 'We'll expect you for dinner, do you hear?'

Camilla stared at them a moment. Paulette, flaunting her hold on Jared by turning a shoulder to her, continued her conversation with him as though Camilla did not exist.

She fought down a quick surge of indignation, murmured, 'Excuse me,' and fled around the corner of the house the way she had come.

Paulette's high peal of laughter sounded clearly; Camilla wondered if it was at her expense. She felt tears of humiliation and anger sting her eyelids, but she brushed them aside as well as her hurt feelings. Soon she would be gone, and would see Jared Kingston and Paulette Fourier no more.

She rushed upstairs to her room, but before she could close the door Selena appeared and asked, 'Are you finished?'

Camilla nodded, not trusting herself to speak and knowing the quick-witted Selena would not miss the tears in her eyes. 'Lawdy, did the horse die?' Selena frowned.

Camilla shook her head. 'No,' she whispered, 'the mare and foal are all right.' She could not look away from the question in those probing dark eyes. She stated flatly, 'I just met Miss Fourier.'

No more explanation seemed necessary for Selena; her eyes narrowed and she glanced knowingly at Camilla. Her gaze swept over her from head to toe, then Selena shook her head and pursed her lips.

'She's no good, that one,' Selena pronounced in disgust.

Camilla turned away wearily and requested, 'Selena, would you fetch water for a bath now, please.'

The door closed gently and Selena was gone after a soft, 'Yes, ma'am.'

Within moments, far sooner than she expected Selena to return, a light tap sounded. Camilla called out permission to enter and the door opened. Jared stood in the doorway, his face expressionless as he announced, 'The Le Meignens are holding a ball within a week. I have tried my utmost to avoid it, but there seems no way to do so; there will be men present whom I need to see. The Le Meignens insist that we come and that I bring you along.'

'Surely I can plead illness,' Camilla demurred.

Jared shook his head. 'No, Governor Claiborne and the Le Meignens are determined to meet you. I suspect,' his voice hardened, 'that Etienne is behind this. At any rate, we are to appear.' His grey eyes went over her. 'I shall fetch a dress-maker and material for a ball gown for you.'

Camilla nodded, too drained to argue or discuss it with him. He closed the door and was gone, but shortly after she had finished her bath and Selena was helping her to dress, a small black woman entered the room.

She spoke to Selena in garbled French, and two girls followed the woman into the room; their arms were loaded with bolts of material which they placed across the bed.

Selena introduced the smaller woman as Jeanerette. The dressmaker studied Camilla thoughtfully, then looked at the girls who stood patiently waiting beside the bed, which was piled high with material, and commanded in perfect English, 'Remove all that. We will not be needing it.'

Without a question the girls loaded their arms once again and left the room. The woman turned to Camilla. 'Let me take your measurements. I shall return tomorrow and fit a dress on you.'

Camilla had to suppress a smile. 'Do I get to select my material?'

Selena stepped forward. 'Ma'am, let the dressmaker make the choice.'

Camilla glanced at her in surprise and guessed that this had been the subject of their discussion a moment earlier. She viewed the thin dark fingers moving swiftly around her waist, measuring the narrow girth. Since the moment she had departed in flight from the President's mansion, nothing in her life had been conventional. A matter of material for a dress was not important enough to take issue with Selena or the dressmaker. She smiled. 'I will look forward to a surprise.'

Selena's face broke into a broad smile, the heartiest one Camilla had received since their first meeting. 'You will not regret it, ma'am,' Selena promised.

CHAPTER
NINE

CAMILLA recalled her words clearly the next day when the dressmaker was once again ushered into her chamber. The woman's helpers followed, carrying a long box between them which they placed on the floor. Selena entered from a side door and closed it behind her. Under the dressmaker's watchful eye, the girls untied thin cords which were wrapped round it and lifted the lid.

Camilla caught her breath at the sight of the shimmering iridescent material. Jeanerette lifted the white gauze dress from the box. It was merely tacked together with the seams lightly basted, but Camilla stared in wonder; never in all her life, not for her presentation, nor for any ball, nor from her Parisian designer, had she ever had or seen anything as beautiful. She gasped with delight, then exclaimed, 'Nothing at the ball could possibly be as lovely!' She raised her eyes and met Selena's gaze.

Selena smiled faintly, and Camilla realised in that moment that she had an ally and staunch friend in the household at Belle Havre. She guessed that Selena had done this to make up for her terrible appearance when she had been introduced to Paulette.

'It is the most beautiful dress I have ever seen anywhere in the world,' Camilla stated sincerely.

'And you will dazzle New Orleans society,' Jeanerette answered with equal sincerity.

Camilla felt the same way about the dress when the night finally arrived. Selena did her hair in two hours of painstaking effort.

As she stared in the ornate mirror at her reflection, Camilla felt she could face the incomparable Paulette without a qualm. Between Selena's laborious efforts and Jeanerette's breathtaking dress she felt well prepared to meet the French girl.

The long-lashed green eyes which stared back at her appeared even more green with the pale dress which was decorated with tiny opals which shimmered against the light.

Her jet-black curls were caught high behind her head and hung down her slender neck, revealing the creamy skin of her throat and shoulders. The lovely reflection in the mirror belied the turmoil which she had experienced the past month.

Camilla descended the sweeping curved staircase to enter the parlour. Jared stood beside a low table which held a decanter of brandy. His back was to her and she slipped quietly into the room, then closed the door. Even as she chided herself for being foolish, her heartbeat quickened at the sight of him. Never had she seen him appear so handsome. The dark blue velvet coat fitted across his broad shoulders with flawless perfection, tapering to his waist over champagne-coloured breeches.

He turned and faced her. The impact of looking into his grey eyes only heightened her feelings. His gaze swept over her slowly from head to toe, then up to meet her eyes, and there was no mistaking the admiration. 'You look lovely,' he declared.

She felt the warmth rush to her cheeks as she thanked him.

'Would you care for anything to drink, brandy, or wine?'

She shook her head and he poured a small amount of brandy for himself, then raised his head to regard her.

'I have news for you; as I understand, your countrymen have some fifty warships ready to descend on New Orleans.' He paused and sipped his drink, then continued, 'There are at least twenty merchant ships in addition, and from what I have heard, there are women on the Admiral's flagship.' His eyes were bright and hard on her. 'The annulment will be settled right away. If I can arrange it, would you like for me to get you to these British ships?'

'Yes,' Camilla replied without feeling. She realised that only last summer her heart would have leapt wildly at such an offer. Now she had no feeling at all. Home was the place to go, but she did not long for it any more.

He gazed at her thoughtfully. 'You do not sound as enthusiastic as I feel you would have at one time.' His eyes went over her once again. 'There are many wealthy men in New Orleans. If you chose to remain, I am certain you would . . .'

Camilla interrupted him, 'I prefer to leave for England at the first possible moment.' She struggled to keep the anger out of her voice. 'I am not searching for a wealthy husband.'

He raised an eyebrow and shrugged, then turned to finish his drink and place the glass on the table.

'Are you ready to leave?' he asked. When she nodded he crossed to take her arm and together they entered the hall where Martin handed Jared a long ice-blue velvet cape for Camilla. Jared's warm fingers brushed her neck lightly as he placed the cape around her shoulders.

Soon they were seated in the carriage and rolling down the lane away from Belle Havre. Camilla asked, 'Do you still expect New Orleans to be invaded?'

'Without any doubt,' he replied. 'General Jackson should reach here any day now. I pray he brings a large number of seasoned troops with him. We are going to be outnumbered beyond all belief.' He added darkly, 'If the men will fight at all.'

'Why would they not fight for the city?'

'New Orleans is a mixture of all kinds of people with many different interests and cultures. Another power taking over the city is a repetition of history which is quite familiar in these parts. The Spanish flag, as well as the French and American flags, has flown over New Orleans during this century.'

'Surely men will fight to save their own homes.'

'We need someone to lead and organise them if that is to happen.' He shifted slightly in the carriage seat to face her better. 'Lafitte has promised his support, and also the Baratarians. Lafitte and I will be able to supply arms and ammunition.'

She was puzzled by his statement and asked, 'Why would you have arms and ammunition in your possession?'

'Last spring Lafitte's brother, Dominique You, made a deal with Mexican patriots to furnish them with weapons. There are many men involved in this, including myself, and consequently we have a large supply of gunpowder and weapons on hand. It has been a lucrative business, for the Mexicans pay in silver. With the long blockade silver is difficult to come by, thus this has been a welcome exchange.' After a moment he added, 'I hope General Jackson will accept what we have to offer.'

'Why would he need to?' Camilla asked.

'He has been fighting with the Greeks and Cherokees in Mississippi Territory, and against the British in Spanish Territory; his supplies may be depleted.'

'In that case why would he not accept what you have with gratitude?' The interior of the carriage was darkening, but she could see his features. He shrugged one shoulder.

'We are privateers—and smugglers. The British have blockaded this port all through the war, although not to the extent that they do now. I have smuggled many goods into New Orleans.'

'And also slaves, I suppose,' she remarked.

'That is Lafitte's enterprise.' His voice hardened. 'I will not deal in slaves.'

'Isn't that a peculiar stand in an area where it is an accepted custom?' Camilla inquired softly.

'Custom be damned!'

She leaned forward, unable to resist asking, 'You must feel quite strongly on the matter?'

'I do,' he replied. 'I do not believe in any man's belonging to another, nor in deception and trickery to gain a hold over another.'

Camilla straightened and turned towards the window. She suspected the last remark had been directed towards herself. Without looking at him she said, 'I did not intend to pry.'

He answered easily, all anger gone from his voice, 'We shall have no quarrels tonight, Mrs Kingston. This is a party; it may be the last for some time.'

The finality of his words conjured up the image of the red glow over the Federal City. 'I pray not,' she said sincerely, and saw his head turn and his eyes rest on her.

'You will be gone soon, back to your precious England. Why would you care?'

'Belle Havre, as well as other plantations, is a beautiful home—it should remain untouched.' She asked, 'How will you get me to the British ships?'

'I do not think it will be difficult if we do so before any fighting commences. I shall try to make arrangements for someone to take you in a boat. I do not think they would fire on a small boat approaching.'

'That sounds risky.'

He startled her by reaching out and grasping her hand lightly. 'Since when have you been afraid of risks?' he asked with amusement.

Before she could answer, he released her hand and leaned back against the seat once more. 'I am teasing you. I will send a man to them under a flag of truce and make arrangements ahead of time. I will not send you forth in such a callous manner.'

Camilla regarded him and realised he was in a good humour for the first time in her presence since the frightful wedding. He became silent, and she turned to view the countryside. Within a short time they passed a large plantation home with a rail fence which bordered the River Road.

The next place was a wide drive flanked by huge spreading oaks which led to the magnificent home of the Fourier family. Its plaster walls gleamed white in the dusk of early evening.

Almost square in design, with a Doric portico and high foundation, it was graced by tall Tuscan columns which added to its grandeur. Jared remarked, 'There is Great Oakes, home of the Fouriers.'

'I know,' she answered, 'Etienne told me.'

'So Etienne has shown you a little of our area.'

Camilla's thoughts were not on the area, or Etienne. 'Do you love her very much?' she asked softly, unable to resist speaking the thing uppermost in her mind.

His head turned and he regarded her steadily. 'When is there love in marriage?'

Camilla's eyes widened; her illusions were shattered with his answer. All this time, she had thought the reason he was not attracted to her as she was to him was because his heart belonged to another. Such was not the case and it came as a shock. Perhaps he had no heart to lose!

How could he not feel what she experienced? she wondered. She had fallen in love with a man who felt nothing in return, not for her or any other woman. She asked, 'You are a wealthy man, surely you are not marrying her for this?' She waved her hand towards the Fourier plantation.

'It will be a satisfactory union. Her family is enormously wealthy, I am well placed also. Together ...' he did not finish, but waved his hand expansively in the air.

She turned away to the window and rode in silence.

'You do not approve,' he remarked.

Camilla faced him. 'It is none of my affair.'

'I must thank you,' he said. 'I would have far sooner, but I have not been home for the past two days, as you well know.'

'I knew no such thing. Thank me for what?'

'For saving my mare and foal. Where did you learn to do such things?'

She shrugged slightly. 'At home.'

'It was an unfortunate meeting between you and Paulette, but then I warned you of her jealous nature. She will not be any more pleasant tonight; most likely she will be a great deal worse.'

'What would cause that?' Camilla asked.

'Do I actually need to tell you? Paulette is accustomed to being the most beautiful girl at any ball she attends. She will not be tonight. Most likely she will behave abominably towards you.'

Camilla's cheeks grew warm. 'It does not matter,' she replied lightly. 'I do not intend to spend my evening chatting with her.'

He laughed softly in the darkness, then said, 'Whenever my ships arrive I will have to leave. If it happens tonight we will return to Belle Havre immediately.'

'Do you expect them?'

'It could be any day now. I appreciate the fact that you have complied with my wishes and not revealed the true time of our marriage, or the fact of my ships arriving.'

She looked at him; the interior of the carriage was darkening in early evening, but she could see his features. 'How do you know I haven't?'

'I would know within the hour,' he stated in a voice that was harsh.

Camilla turned away and rode in silence. Later, Jared remarked, 'We are passing Versailles Plantation; it is the home of Pierre Denis de la Ronde. You should meet him tonight. Has Etienne showed you that too?'

'Yes,' Camilla answered.

'And I imagine he has told you about it. It was built to establish some of the magnificence of its namesake. I see Etienne has kept you entertained.'

'I have enjoyed his company,' she replied with honesty.

They both became silent. Camilla sat with her head turned towards the window, staring out at the dark while she thought about sailing for home within a short time. She looked at Jared and asked, 'Did you send my letter to my solicitor?'

He replied, 'Of course not, there is no way for me to send it at the moment.'

'Then why did you take it?' Camilla inquired.

'I did it to see if there actually was a solicitor.'

She bit back a remark about his intentions and turned to the window once again and they continued the drive without further conversation. Finally the carriage turned into a winding alley of pines which led to a large home blazing with lights. The early Colonial house, with its wooden colonettes and exterior stairs beneath the galleries, was bathed in yellow light which spilled from the windows as well as illumination from flaming torches placed along the drive.

The flickering orange glow from the torches reflected in the carriage. For an instant before the door was opened by a slave, Camilla looked into Jared's eyes. Then the door opened and Jared stepped down, turned and reached up to take her hand. As they approached the house, he looked down at her and remarked, 'Your hands are like ice.'

Camilla ignored his remark and within seconds he added, 'You are afraid.'

She looked up quickly. 'Why wouldn't I be?'

'It is easy to understand why I am less than happy about our appearance together,' he replied, 'it will be awkward for Paulette as well as for me. But I did not think you would feel this way.'

'I am a curiosity to the people who know you,' Camilla declared. 'Surely you realised that when you insisted that I attend?'

His grey eyes were unreadable, gazing with a curious intensity into her own. 'I am certain Etienne was the cause of all the insistence on your being here.' He added drily, 'I assumed that you had put the idea into his head.'

'Why on earth would I do such a thing?' she asked with feeling, then realised just as quickly, 'Ah, so you still think I attempted to trick you into marriage and would be happy to appear anywhere at your side as your wife!' She halted and faced him. 'I wonder at what point in your life you will realise the truth—or trust anyone other than yourself?'

She suffered the probing scrutiny of his eyes, then Jared took her arm once again. 'Come, they are waiting on us.'

At the door a butler accepted their things, then they stepped forward to be greeted by the host and hostess, the Le Meignens.

Mrs Le Meignen squeezed Camilla's hand and welcomed her warmly. The small woman smiled with a face framed by white curls. 'I am so happy to meet you. How beautiful you look, my dear.'

Camilla murmured a thank-you, looking down at Mrs Le Meignen and finding only sincerity in the pale blue eyes which gazed up at her in return. Mrs Le Meignen patted Camilla's hand and added, 'Later, when our guests have arrived, I want to get better acquainted with you.'

'I would like that very much,' Camilla replied, then turned as Mrs Le Meignen released her hand to greet Jared. She clasped his hands as he leaned down and kissed her cheek. 'My dear boy, how good it is to see you. It seems you have been away from here for years.'

'I am glad to be home,' he replied.

She smiled up at him. 'You must come see the new horses.'

'And you must come see mine.'

Mrs Le Meignen's eyes darted quickly from Jared to Camilla, then she told him, 'I am happy you both came tonight.'

'We will talk in a while,' Jared promised, then took Camilla's arm and they strolled towards the ballroom. He remarked, 'She meant what she said to you.'

She studied him with curiosity. 'They must be close friends of yours.'

'They are, or I never would have succumbed to their insistence that we both appear at this ball.'

The music grew louder as they neared the dance floor with a rollicking tune which was unfamiliar to Camilla. When they stepped inside the door of the ballroom they paused while Jared scanned the throng of guests. Under huge crystal chandeliers groups of dancers followed lively steps. The pale green plastered walls were a backdrop for the many baskets of flowers and ferns. With all the candles and the crowd, the glass doors were thrown open to the veranda; the beauty of the room was heightened by fan transoms above each door.

'What tune do they play?' Camilla asked.

He looked down and smiled. 'I suspect you are not accustomed to our country dances; I think you will find this quite different from your staid Washington parties.'

Camilla had little time to reflect on his comments. She became aware of the increasing attention they were receiving as more and more of the guests noticed their entrance. As so many eyes stared in their direction Camilla felt drained of strength; she was too conscious of the faces studying them and of the fact that she stood at the side of a man whom everybody knew wanted to be free of her.

Her gaze swept across the crowd seeing no familiar face, then was caught by one pair of lovely blue eyes which were so clearly filled with venom that there could be no mistaking it.

Paulette Fourier, surrounded by four handsome men, gazed at Camilla with pure hatred. She was looking as lovely as she had the last time they had met, the deep-wine velvet dress set off her exquisite beauty and heightened the flush which rose to her cheeks at the sight of her. Then, as a clear insult, she deliberately turned her back towards Jared and Camilla to commence talking again with her companions.

Camilla felt as if a million pairs of hostile eyes bored into her, then Etienne parted from a group and crossed to greet them, and the feeling was gone.

He bowed over her hand, then greeted Jared. 'I have been watching for your arrival.'

Jared smiled wryly and his glance flicked over the crowd. 'I feel you were not the only one. Have you heard any word of General Jackson, Etienne?'

Etienne shrugged shoulders clad in soft grey-green velvet. 'No. He is expected any time now, but he did not arrive today.'

'Good evening,' the high-pitched childish voice carried clearly as Paulette joined them. Her eyes rested on Camilla and she uttered a brief, 'Evening.'

Camilla smiled. 'Good evening, Miss Fourier.'

Paulette looked at Jared and remarked, 'I see, Jared, that you have finally purchased a dress for your wife.' Her eyes slid to Camilla. 'How pretty she is without straw in her hair.' Without allowing time for Camilla to reply, Paulette tapped Jared's arm with her folded fan. 'I have held this first dance for you as I promised, and much to my regret. Had I known how long you would keep me waiting I would never have done so.'

He smiled and turned to Camilla, but before he could speak Etienne said, 'And I will claim this dance with Camilla.'

The two men exchanged a glance, then Jared murmured, 'Excuse me, my dear,' and took Paulette's arm to step to the dance floor.

Camilla looked up at Etienne who stared after the couple. His brow was creased in a frown. 'One cannot call out a woman, but I certainly would like to.'

Camilla laughed. 'I am not worried by her remarks. They are of no importance to me tonight.'

Etienne swept her into his arms for a waltz. 'No, you need not be concerned; you are the loveliest female here tonight. Paulette is seething with jealous rage. She is not accustomed to anyone overshadowing her or taking attention from her.'

Camilla laughed. 'That is foolishness, Etienne.'

'Indeed not,' he answered solemnly, 'I fear I will not have you to myself for long.'

His words turned out to be true, as first one handsome man and then another wanted introductions, and claimed dances with Camilla until Jared returned to her side.

'I see you are taking New Orleans society by storm,' he remarked.

'I think not.'

'Come, I have someone I want you to meet.' He took her arm and steered her through the throng to introduce her to Governor William Claiborne and his wife. Within minutes the men were discussing matters of war, then Jared took her hand to lead her back to the dance floor.

She gazed up at him while they danced. 'You seem to be on better terms with the Governor than I would have guessed from all your remarks.'

'Our relations are not as strained now as they were a while back. I am more discreet in my activities than the Lafittes. As my sugar plantation grows, the privateering lessens.'

They whirled in a half-circle and Camilla saw Paulette's smouldering eyes on them.

'You do not have to dance with me. I think Miss Fourier would appreciate it if you did not.'

'Do you think I would dance with you if I did not want to?'

Camilla averted her head from his unblinking scrutiny. He asked, 'What will you do when you return to England?'

She shrugged slightly. 'I have been so concerned with returning that I have not considered it.' She looked up at him. 'What does anyone do when they return home? I shall take up my life again as I left it.'

He raised his head and stared into space. 'I shall have to make arrangements for you to leave soon; if the British invade we will have little opportunity to get you away safely.'

The dance ended and Etienne claimed the next, his blue eyes filled unmistakably with admiration for Camilla. In a sea of dark velvets her gauze dress shone with a springlike delicacy which stood out like a white orchid on a bed of greenery. Amidst all the dark French and Spanish descendants, the lovely Creole women, Camilla's fair skin set her apart as much as her pale dress.

She was the centre of attention and the time passed swiftly, until at the end of one dance she turned to gaze into Jared's eyes. He reached for her hand. 'I shall not allow you to decline this next dance with me.'

His white teeth flashed and for an instant she recalled that moment in Boisblanc's cabin when he had been so relaxed and contented. 'Of course.' She smiled up at him and allowed him to lead her on to the floor.

'You have captivated the hearts of half the men of New Orleans society.'

She laughed at his remark. 'Ridiculous, sir!'

He did not laugh in return, but gazed intently into her eyes. 'If you have taken a liking to New Orleans and would prefer to live here, I am certain that within a short time you would have offers of marriage from the most eligible men in the world, as soon as the annulment is finalised.'

Her gaiety faded and she stared up at him, lost in his unfathomable look. 'I shall leave New Orleans at the first possible moment.'

They looked into each other's eyes and something passed between them. Camilla forgot that anything or anyone existed except the man before her. She followed his steps mechanically, moving in time to the music, but hearing nothing except the tumultuous beating of her own heart.

'You are lovely,' he said softly.

'Thank you,' she replied. She could not look away, then without conscious thought she glanced at his mouth, and just as rapidly blushed in recollection.

He whirled her through the wide doors on to the veranda. The night was cool, but not too much to be uncomfortable as they danced away from the ballroom into the shadows. Suddenly he halted and stared down at her, then his arms closed around her and pulled her to him. He lowered his head and his lips brushed hers gently, searchingly.

Camilla knew she should make him stop, should attempt to push away, even though there would be no way to prevent it if he intended to hold her. But she did nothing except remain still, her face raised to his as his lips moved on hers.

And she knew she was hopelessly lost. Her arms entwined around his neck and she yielded herself to him as his kiss deepened; the tenderness changed to passion—to a scalding touch which she returned fully.

She could not hide her response, or the terrible longing she had kept hidden since their journey together, which seemed so long ago.

He raised his head a fraction to study her; when he spoke his voice was low and filled with curiosity. 'Your inhibitions are gone; something has changed you ...'

Camilla moved to get away. 'Please ...'

He pulled her into his arms again to kiss her once more, and all her resistance melted away immediately.

In spite of the forced marriage and annulment, in spite of his hateful words and cold treatment, she loved him with all her heart and she could not resist his passionate kisses, even though she knew there was no love in them.

Her head tilted back on her slender neck as his arms crushed her tightly against the length of his hard body.

'Jared!' a high voice called, repeating the name insistently.

Instantly he released Camilla and she turned to face Paulette. For a second she looked into blue eyes filled with rage, then she ran across the veranda towards the steps.

Behind her, Jared spoke Paulette's name, then his words faded as Camilla raced down the steps and away from the house.

When she reached the shelter of pines in the yard she slowed, gasping for breath. She closed her eyes an instant, remembering the touch of his lips against hers. 'I love you,' she whispered to the darkness, and let tears spill unheeded across her cheeks.

She strolled among box hedges trimmed in formal array. A summerhouse stood at one end of the garden, and she sauntered on without giving thought to direction. Near the structure, under a tall pine, was a marble bench. Camilla stepped into dark shadows and sat down on it to let the tears flow.

Finally she wiped her cheeks, knowing that she could not return to the ballroom until she was composed and her eyes were no longer red. She rose and strolled through the summer house, looking at the exotic blooming plants which were sheltered under glass and held a soft lustrous beauty in the moonlight.

She returned to the darkened bench and sat once again. She had no inclination to return to the ballroom and the dancing. The evening had changed; she did not care to face Jared again, or watch him hold Paulette in his arms while they danced.

As if the very thought of her conjured up the real person, Paulette's childish voice was heard clearly. She was approaching with someone, and Camilla guessed it could only be Jared.

She did not care to encounter either one of them. In a moment of panic she rose to her feet to flee and realised she was trapped by the thick hedges, the summerhouse behind her and their approach down the lane ahead of her. Without thinking she slipped behind the pine and gathered her skirts close about her legs, praying that she would not be discovered and that they would walk on.

'My darling!' Paulette spoke quickly. 'We are alone at last!'

There was a long moment of silence. Camilla closed her eyes and leaned against the rough trunk of the tree in the painful realisation that the silence must signify that Jared was kissing Paulette, just as he had kissed her only little less than an hour ago.

She squeezed her eyes closed more tightly, wishing she were any place else on earth; she tried to close her mind to what was happening right at hand.

'My darling!' Paulette breathed.

'*Je t'aime, je t'adore!*' a masculine voice replied.

Camilla's eyes opened wide with shock. There was no mistaking that the voice she had just heard, the deep male voice declaring his love, was not that of Jared Kingston.

CHAPTER
TEN

CAMILLA stared into the darkness and longed to peer around the tree and discover the man's identity, but she dared not risk them finding her. Once again they were silent, then when they began to talk she listened to the man's fluent French, spoken in a hushed voice but still audible at such close range. The man to whom Paulette was declaring her love was not Jared Kingston.

Emotions rose in Camilla, shock at the discovery of Paulette's deceit, as well as relief and wonder.

Paulette said, 'Come, my darling. I know a place more private; someone may come here because we are close to the house.'

They hurried away, and in a minute all was silent once again and Camilla stepped cautiously from behind the pine. She had forgotten her tears. Lost in contemplation of the scene she had just overheard, she wandered in the direction of the house.

As she approached the steps a figure moved from the shadows on the veranda. 'Camilla!' Etienne called softly.

She answered and watched him hurry forward to meet her. 'I have searched the place over for you.' He walked into the moonlight and she could see the frown on his brow. He looked past her into the darkness of the gardens behind her. 'Are you wandering around alone out here?'

'Yes, I'm afraid so,' she answered easily.

'I shall remedy that. Do you want to continue your stroll?' Without waiting for her answer he took her arm and fell into step beside her. They ambled slowly in the direction of the front of the house.

'Etienne, do you think Jared loves Paulette?'

His answer was soft. 'No, I do not think Jared will allow himself to love any woman in the sense you mean. There have been many broken hearts—but not his.'

She smiled wryly in the darkness. 'Do you think Paulette is in love with him?' She looked up at Etienne.

He shrugged. 'I suppose so; she would not be alone.'

'Suppose she does not love him, that she is in love with someone else. Would it matter to Jared?'

'I imagine he would call the man out and kill him if she would do such a thing after they are officially engaged or wed. I do not think Paulette is that foolish. She knows Jared's disposition and his ability as a marksman.'

They strolled in silence past beds of late-blooming autumn flowers, walking towards the brightly lighted front of the big house. Before they reached the corner, while they were still on the dark side, Etienne reached out and caught her arm, turning her to face him.

'Camilla, the annulment will be settled this week.'

'I guessed as much from what you said last Thursday.'

He looked down at her. 'I wish you would reconsider leaving New Orleans.'

She shook her head. 'My mind is made up. I have waited a long time to return home.'

He stepped closer and folded her gently in his arms, then he bent down and kissed her tenderly. His arms tightened and pulled her close.

Camilla reached up and placed her arms against the velvet sleeves of his coat, aware of his kiss, but far more aware of the difference in her feelings between this embrace and the one earlier with Jared.

He raised his head to look down at her. 'Camilla . . .'

She reached up quickly and laid her fingers against his lips. 'Etienne, do not say more. I can do nothing else but go. It is useless to discuss, and will only be painful.'

She moved her hand away and looked imploringly at him. He stared at her a moment in silence, then whispered, 'Jared?'

She stood quite still. Etienne whispered, 'Are you in love with him?'

She could not deny it. Etienne groaned and dropped his arms to turn away. She stared at his back, then reached forward and touched him lightly. 'Etienne, I am sorry . . .'

He faced her. 'Camilla, if you would be my wife, I would move anywhere you would like to live. We could go where you would never see Jared Kingston again and I would do all in my power to make you forget him.'

'Etienne, please,' she begged, 'I cannot. Do not do this to yourself. I am certain I am not the girl for you, else I would feel the same way. Etienne, thank you. I shall always remember.'

'Camilla, please . . .'

'I cannot,' she cried. 'I cannot help what I feel!'

He was silent for a time, then he said quietly, 'Damn his soul.'

'Do not say that,' she whispered through the darkness. 'He is your friend, and he did nothing to encourage such feelings from me. He does not even know how I feel.'

'Then he is an absolute fool,' Etienne declared bitterly.

'It is useless. Soon I will leave here, and you will forget.'

'Never!' He reached out and pulled her into his arms to hold her close; her cheek was pressed against the soft velvet of his coat. He placed his head against hers and stood quietly. When he spoke his voice was harsh and deep. 'Camilla, if you ever change your mind, or need me . . . I shall always be at your call . . .'

She pulled away slightly and gazed up at him with her hands lightly against his chest. 'Etienne, you are wonderful—and some day you will forget all about me.' She raised on tiptoe and kissed him on the cheek, then took his hand. 'We should go in now.'

He moved beside her without a word. When they entered

the lighted ballroom, he took her in his arms to waltz. The music was loud, filling the room with melody. Camilla gazed up at Etienne's face and felt a twist in her heart.

If only she could love this gentle man! He had many fine qualities; for one fleeting second she considered the possibility of marriage to him.

It would be peaceful and secure; he would always be considerate of her. Then he led her in a sweeping turn and she met the disturbing stare which always seemed to see into her very soul. Jared stood at the edge of the dance floor across the room, but for a moment their glances caught and held and the familiar quickening of her heart told her how utterly useless it would ever be to consider marriage to any other man.

She sighed, a small forlorn exhaling, and Etienne looked down at her solemnly. 'You are the most beautiful woman here.'

'Thank you.' She could barely summon the words, hating to gaze into his eyes and read their message. The waltz ended and another began; Etienne held fast to her hand and had commenced once more to dance with her when Jared appeared at her elbow to tell her it was time to leave.

She squeezed Etienne's hand before they parted, feeling as if she were squeezing her own heart. She could not bear the pain she saw in his eyes.

As soon as they were seated and moving in the carriage Jared turned to face her and said, 'My ships will be in right away. I must get home.'

'I was quite ready to leave,' she answered, acutely aware of his presence.

In a quick movement he slid on to the seat beside her and took her in his arms. 'Camilla . . .'

'Please . . .' she pushed against him, hating her heart for pounding so violently.

His voice was soft against her ear as he kissed her throat. 'You do not want me to leave.'

With a violent thrust she pushed away and moved to the opposite seat of the carriage. 'Please, leave me alone!'

He answered quietly, 'Very well.'

They stared at each other a moment, then Camilla turned away to look out the window at the darkness while she calmed her shattered nerves.

They rode a long time in silence until finally she turned to him and asked, 'Will it take long for you to reach your ships?'

'Yes, I have a lengthy ride, which is why we needed to leave immediately. The ships come in down the coast, away from the authorities' prying eyes, but it takes longer for me to get there and it is more difficult to handle unloading.' He sighed heavily and spoke in an impersonal tone, for which she was relieved.

'Everything is happening at a bad time,' he remarked, 'but then I guess wars never wait for a good time.'

'What else is going on?' she asked.

'It is time for a frost. We need to harvest before a killing frost, to get the cane converted to muscovados.'

'What are muscovados?'

'Blocks of unrefined or raw sugar. It is time now to cut the canes, then they will be crushed by rollers and the juice boiled, the molasses drained. I hope we can get through the harvest without interference and get the hogsheads loaded to ship for market.'

'If you have so much to do at home and have such a large plantation, why do you deal in smuggling?'

'It used to be necessary; that is how I built the plantation.'

'Will you be away long?'

'Perhaps a week. Instruct Selena to pack your things. I will make arrangements while I am gone and as soon as I return I will get you to a ship if possible.' He added in a curious tone, 'If that is what you want.'

'Yes. The annulment will be final this week.'

'I know,' he replied.

'When is your wedding?'

He sighed. 'We have made no plans; that will have to wait. It will be less awkward for Paulette if I do not go from an annulment immediately to the altar.'

Camilla looked away and rode quietly without further conversation. When they once again entered Belle Havre Jared issued instructions to Martin to help him get ready to leave. Jared's valet, a tall muscular black named Armaud, stood ready at the head of the stairs and immediately went on an errand at Jared's direction. Camilla ignored the commotion and strolled to her own room. Selena had turned down the bed and left one small lamp glowing in readiness for Camilla's return. One of the long glass doors which opened on to the second floor gallery, was ajar and Camilla crossed to close it. No sooner had she finished than she heard a rap on the door; at her command it opened and Jared entered. He closed the door and leaned against it to gaze at her.

'You look very beautiful tonight,' he said.

'Thank you,' she replied warily, curious as to what was on his mind.

He crossed to her and Camilla felt her pulse quicken at his nearness. He stood in front of her and gazed down at her a moment, then pulled her to him and leaned down to kiss her.

She was no more able to tell him to stop than she had been earlier in the evening. All rational thought and cold logic fled at his touch. She melted into his arms and returned his kiss until he raised his head and looked into her eyes.

For one fleeting instant Camilla thought he might declare his love. Her hopes rose that he would say he no longer wanted the annulment. Why else would he come to her room to take her in his arms when he was in a rush to leave Belle Havre to reach his ships?

Then with damning clarity he revealed his intentions. He tilted her chin up and looked into her eyes. 'Camilla, there is no need for you to return to England if you do not want to.'

She was aware of his use for the first time of her Christian name, and her heart quickened at his words. He continued softly, 'I am willing to get you a house in New Orleans. I would pay for everything as long as you wish to stay.'

For an instant she hoped he would declare his love, then

she realised what he was saying—that he was willing to make her his mistress.

All the hurt and humiliation she had suffered at his hands went into the resounding blow as she slapped his cheek. He caught her hands quickly; she struggled to get free from him. 'Let me go!' she cried.

His eyes narrowed. 'What the devil was that for? You know I am not going to remain married to you. What did you expect when you returned my kisses in such a manner?'

'Get out of this room immediately!' she hissed at him and yanked her wrists free of his grasp. 'Please go!'

He caught one wrist and prevented her from getting away from him. 'Answer me! What did you expect when you returned my kisses like that?'

'Let go of me! I will never answer your question! Your ships are waiting—go now!' She glared at him feeling angry and hurt at the same time.

'I cannot understand you.' His eyes searched her face, and Camilla closed her own to shut out his countenance and his keen observation.

'How many times must I ask you to leave?' she whispered.

He released her wrist and declared quietly, 'I am sorry if I offended you, but from your response you indicated . . .'

'I regret anything you think I indicated,' she interrupted, 'but will you just go?'

He turned on his heel and was gone in an instant, leaving her utterly defeated and forlorn.

Within a short time she heard hoofbeats on the drive, then all grew quiet and she knew he was gone. Camilla slipped off the beautiful dress and hung it up, then donned her white nightgown. Long after she climbed into bed she lay awake staring into the darkness with her thoughts in a turmoil over all that had happened during the evening.

She slept only a few hours, then rose to ask Selena to have the portmanteau fetched. She had few things and it would be little effort to pack to get ready to leave. The days passed without sign of Jared or any news of the British. Martin and Armaud both had gone with Jared, so the house was quieter than usual. One afternoon she was seated in the library and heard voices in the hall. Camilla rose and opened the door to step into the hallway, and faced Paulette Fourier talking with Selena.

'Good afternoon,' Camilla said. As soon as she spoke Selena turned and left.

Miss Fourier's blue eyes narrowed; she smoothed the folds of a dark blue velvet cape as she spoke. 'Is Jared home?'

'No,' Camilla replied.

Paulette took a deep breath, then said, 'Very well. He said you would be leaving right away.'

'I intend to.'

Paulette's eyes flicked across the empty hall, then rested once more on Camilla. 'I am sure you will be much happier away from here, Miss Hyde.'

'Do not worry, Miss Fourier, I shall soon be out of his life.'

Paulette's chin tilted upwards. 'I am not in the least concerned. Jared wants you gone, and he will see to it you are. You have caused him a great deal of difficulty and embarrassment and it has gained you nothing. The sooner you are gone, the happier he will be.'

'You have made your point,' Camilla stated, 'I see no need to continue this conversation.'

'No, except be aware, Miss Hyde, I will not allow anything to interfere with my future as mistress of Belle Havre.' Her blue eyes glittered with malice. 'The annulment is final, you know. I think it would have been sooner, except that Etienne wanted to keep you here. You are no longer Jared's wife—not even in name only,' she declared with vicious delight. 'Furthermore, Jared has promised me that you would not spend one night under this roof once the annulment was final.'

'I see no need to continue this talk, Miss Fourier.'

Paulette turned on her heel and hurried through the front door. Camilla stared after her, wondering how Jared could ever hope for a happy life with such a woman at his side, but then she realised that Paulette would never act in that manner with him.

She returned to the library to read; the Sunday afternoon passed slowly with no sign of Jared or anyone else other than the usual servants. When Camilla entered her room that night she found Selena had turned down the covers and lighted the lamps. Her white gown and blue robe were laid out on the bed, but after Camilla had changed into the gown and climbed into bed to read, she found it difficult to keep her mind on the book.

She roused and realised that she had dozed off with the lamps still burning. She climbed down out of bed to extinguish them when she heard a commotion on the drive, then Jared's voice rang out clearly. She stepped to the window to gaze below. The men were mounted on horseback milling in front of the house; Jared dismounted and the others led his horse away as he turned and entered the house.

She longed to run downstairs and greet him, even after the terrible scene before their parting, but there was no more to say to each other and she knew she could not do so. She returned to the bed and lifted the book in her hands without seeing the words.

His boots sounded loudly in the hall, then halted, and he knocked. Against all reason her heart quickened. She slipped out of bed and pulled on the blue organdy robe, then called for him to enter.

He opened the door, stepped inside and closed it behind him. Clad in mud-spattered hessians, dusty leather breeches and coat, with a heavy beard, he appeared happier than he had in some time.

'You have unloaded your ships!' she exclaimed.

He crossed to stand close before her, his eyes going over her long black curls which tumbled about her shoulders. Camilla pulled the robe closer under her chin as he viewed her from head to toe.

'I am glad it was successful; you look quite happy.'

'I have to leave right away,' he told her.

Camilla guessed, 'The British have attacked?'

He nodded. 'General Jackson is here. I met with him briefly tonight. He received word two days ago that early in the morning on December fourteenth, five American gunboats were caught between Malheureux Island and Point Claire on the mainland. The British had a flotilla of forty-five barges, which had pursued the gunboats for two days until they caught up with them and engaged in a fight. Ten Americans were killed during the battle; the gunboats and men were captured and taken to Cat Island, which has given the British command of Lake Borgne.' He paused, then added, 'The battle for New Orleans will commence soon now.'

'Must you go tonight?' When he nodded she asked, 'Did you eat dinner earlier?'

'No, I was in a hurry to return home. I will eat before I leave. Camilla . . .'

She interrupted, saying, 'You must be tired from travelling. Surely you can wait to leave until morning.'

'Camilla . . .' He closed the distance between them. She started to move away, but he reached out quickly and caught her hands in his.

She looked up at him. 'Please . . . we have said everything that can be said.'

He shrugged out of his coat and tossed it on to a chair without ever taking his eyes off her, and holding continually to first one hand and then the other as he pulled off the garment.

He shook his head at her statement. 'No, we have not said everything that can be . . .' His voice was soft; he pulled her closer as he uttered the words, then his arms went around her and he leaned down to kiss her.

CHAPTER
ELEVEN

CAMILLA felt drowned in longing. All her resolutions to not allow him to kiss her again dissolved instantly at his touch. With all the yearning and love she felt for him she returned his kiss until she realised that she would have to make him stop or be beyond a point to resist at all.

She placed both hands against his chest and pushed until he released her slightly. 'You must not!' she cried.

His grey eyes seemed to darken and devour her. His voice was husky. 'Camilla—I am in love with you.'

She could only stare in disbelief at him. His arms closed around her and pulled her close while he gazed down tenderly.

'I have been the worst sort of fool. I have fought my own feelings and I did not acknowledge what I felt, or realise it until I was away from here and faced with the fact that you would be leaving for ever.'

She regarded him with amazement while he talked. She had dreamed of such a declaration, and then seen her hopes crushed until she had given up all thought of any possibility that he would ever feel anything for her.

'I could not wait to return to tell you,' he said. 'I would have left my ships and come home sooner except for the fact that we were in danger, and I knew you could not leave until I was back.' His voice deepened. 'I love you, Camilla, I want you to be my wife.'

She looked up at him. 'And suppose I marry you for your wealth?'

He smiled. 'I would not give a damn.' With an arm holding

her close he ran his finger along her chin. 'It does not matter; I am hopelessly in love with you.'

Camilla's heart leapt. 'I love you . . .' she breathed. He crushed her to him then, his mouth seeking hers. His lips came gently against hers, moving, shifting.

Camilla wrapped her arms around his neck and clung to him, unable to comprehend fully that he truly did love her, except for the burning kisses he was showering on her. Her senses reeled in ecstasy and she returned kiss for kiss with rising passion.

Once he pulled away slightly and looked down at her. 'I have ridden hard all day; you will be covered with dust and dirt . . .'

She interrupted, 'How could I care about that?'

His arms tightened once more and he kissed her again. With his lips on hers he placed his arm under her knees and swung her easily into his arms to cross the few yards to the bed.

He lowered her to the bed gently. His mouth was pressed to hers while his hands worked at the fastenings of the blue robe. He peeled the robe off her arms slowly and let it fall to the bed.

He pulled her into his arms and cradled her head against his shoulder while he kissed her. The shining curls which shimmered in the lamp's glow, were spread across his shoulder. He stroked the silky tresses, then followed the curve of her slender throat to untie the ribbons of her gown.

For a moment he released her, and Camilla opened her eyes and sat up facing him. She could not take her eyes from his; the grey depths were filled with unspoken desire. With a swift movement Jared tugged his shirt free and pulled it off to drop it on the floor. His bronze skin rippled with muscles across his chest and powerful shoulders.

He reached out and gathered the open neck of her gown in his hand to slide it off her shoulders. Her eyes widened as she stared into his, while he moved the soft material to drop it around her waist. His eyes lowered, looking at her, then ifted. With a groan he pulled her into his arms again. She lay back in his embrace, sliding her hands over the hard muscles of his arms as he held her.

His eyes moving over her body were as searing as his touch; the desire for her leapt and flamed in them. He crushed her against him and kissed her hungrily; his flesh was warm against hers, while his tongue was burning, evoking a wild response from her.

His hand slid down her throat to her breast with caresses which heightened her passion, and Camilla's senses reeled from his touch. Her body arched in his arms, straining against him as she returned his hungry kisses with wild abandon.

He bent over her slowly, and together they sank to the bed with his weight heavy on top of her. She lay pinned under him with her arms wrapped around his broad shoulders; she was lost utterly. She could do nothing but yield because she was his for ever, heart and soul, in whatever manner he wanted her.

She was unable to push him away, but could only cling to him and whisper, 'I love you, Jared . . .'

He moved to lay beside her and hold her against him. His hand cupped her breast, then caressed her while he kissed her throat; his tongue was a flame against her flesh. He kissed her with deliberation across the soft skin of her throat, down to her breasts.

Camilla moaned softly in pleasure, tightening her arms round his neck. He raised slightly, and as she gazed into his eyes there could be no doubts as to his feelings for her.

She tugged against his shoulders to pull him down once again, then looked up in surprise as he resisted and straightened over her. He grasped her slender arms with his hands and stared at her, his voice a rasp as he spoke. 'It will not be this way.'

Camilla stared at him. 'You do not want marriage?' she asked in a small voice.

He exhaled quickly. 'My love . . .' His words broke off as

he pulled her to him. 'Of course I want marriage, if you will have me after all I have put you through.' He pulled away slightly. 'Camilla, will you be my wife?'

'Yes! Oh, yes . . .'

He kissed her passionately, then declared, 'We will do this right.' He sobered as he looked at her. 'You shall have a wedding, and not remember for all of your life that terrible night and my tyrannical, foolish actions.'

His voice deepened and became tender; he caught the fold of the gown and pulled it up over her shoulders while he talked. 'Camilla, you shall have a lovely wedding in a church, one to remember always.' His eyes changed, burning into hers. 'And then we shall have a wedding night you will never forget. I shall wipe that night at Mobile from your mind forever.'

'Jared,' she whispered, 'I love you. You do not have to wait . . .'

He closed his eyes, then crushed her in his arms for another long passionate kiss. Suddenly he released her and rose to his feet. 'No, I meant what I said. You deserve far better than that and I want you to be able always to remember our wedding as a time of joy.' He grinned down at her. 'My timing has been quite poor. The annulment is final and you are no longer my wife.'

'Are you certain?' she asked.

'Yes, but it would not matter.' His grin faded. 'I want you to have a proper wedding.'

She reached out and caught his hand. 'I do not want to wait!'

He raised her hand to his lips and kissed first the back of her hand, then turned it palm up to cover the warm flesh with lingering kisses. 'No, because I am filthy from my journey and I am due in New Orleans right now. I will make arrangements and it will be as soon as possible. I will send Jeanerette to fashion a wedding dress. I must go, Camilla . . .'

She looked up at him and asked quickly, 'You said you had not eaten, will you please do that before you go?'

He leaned down to kiss her. 'You know where I would rather spend any time while I am here.'

'Please,' she begged, 'you do not know what you will be doing tomorrow, and it may be a long time before you have another meal. Please, Jared, I will worry less . . .'

'Very well. Come sit with me. I want to change first; tell Berry to cook something while I clean up.' He added, 'And ask him to hurry.'

The moment Jared left the room Camilla slipped into the robe and tugged the bell-pull. As soon as Selena appeared she asked her to summon the cook and prepare dinner for Jared. Selena nodded and left, then Camilla turned to brush her hair.

She viewed her reflection; her cheeks were flushed beneath her wide green eyes with her full lips red from Jared's kisses. She tugged the brush slowly through her hair, allowing the shining tresses to straighten then spring back into curl. When she finished the brushing, she fastened her gown and robe, then descended to the dining-room to wait for Jared.

He was quick to appear, washed and in clean clothes. The candles on the table gave a soft glow to the room. As soon as his dinner was served the servant departed, leaving them alone. Jared placed his fork in his plate and caught her hand to pull her nearer. 'I am not hungry for this dinner,' he declared, and leaned forward to kiss her.

After a moment Camilla pulled away from him. 'Please, you promised me you would eat.'

He smiled at her. 'Are you going to be a nagging wife?'

She returned his smile. 'Perhaps.'

He squeezed her hand and held it on his knee while he commenced to eat.

'Jared,' she waited until he looked at her, then continued, 'I did not know I would meet Edward Searles. I was not trying to trap you into marriage, that was the last thing I would have expected.'

'Camilla, I can never apologise enough for my actions, and you need not make any explanations.' He paused to sip his wine, then lowered the glass and looked at her.

'My love, when I was young—just nineteen, to be exact—my father died, leaving me his heir as the elder son. I was quite inexperienced. I also had a younger step-brother, who . . .' he paused a moment, then said, 'hated me. I stood in the way of an inheritance.

'It is a long, shabby story, but I was tricked, trapped by a girl and her unscrupulous mother into one of those situations which is compromising according to our society, yet actually amounts to nothing. I refused to be trapped into a marriage I did not want at such an age, merely because I had been with the girl late at night and unchaperoned; I would not do the gentlemanly thing and marry her.'

He paused to sip the wine, then continued, 'Her father called me out, and it came down to either fighting a duel with the man or marrying his daughter. I chose the duel, being hot-headed and young. He made it clear that it would not merely be a duel to draw blood, but to death.'

His voice grew harsher as he talked and related. 'I was a good shot, although there was no certainty about the outcome, for the father had a reputation as an excellent marksman. I received a message from my second to meet him early at the appointed place. I rode out to do so, and arrived to find myself alone with the corpse of the girl's father. He had been shot and killed only minutes before I arrived.'

Camilla exclaimed, 'How dreadful!'

'To this day I do not know with certainty who did it. The possibility always existed that brigands set upon him, although I have always doubted it. I summoned the constable, and we soon discovered that the note I had received was not sent by my second. I was accused by the hysterical girl and her mother of having murdered the man in order to prevent the duel.' He paused once more to sip his wine. His grey eyes were opaque and brooding as he stared into space.

'The evidence was damning; I was hauled away to New-gate. My step-brother moved swiftly. He saw to it that I could deal only with him. The more time that passed, the worse conditions and my case became.

'My step-brother appeared one afternoon; he had bribed the jailer and spent all afternoon in discussion with me, and I finally agreed to his proposal. In exchange for my free-dom—which he would see to—I would allow him to bribe the jailer and have me officially declared dead. Then he would be the heir. I had to sign a paper confessing I murdered the girl's father and promise I would leave England and never return. I agreed, because it was that or hang.'

'How terrible,' Camilla whispered. She placed her free hand over his and he quickly clasped both of hers in his grasp. He spoke harshly.

'That was bad enough, but he made it worse. He did not live up to his part of the bargain. At the coast, when I reached a ship and before I could sail, I was to sign everything over to him. He was taking no chances. I did not know until he was gone that he had made an arrangement with the ship's captain.

'I was transported to one of Spain's colonies and sold into bondage there.'

She regarded him with shock. 'Then that is why you will not own slaves,' she said.

He nodded. 'It is also why I prey on Spanish ships. I escaped within the year, but it was a bitter lesson and one I can never forget.' His eyes softened and roamed over her countenance. 'You see why I was so fearful of a conniving female attempting to lure me into marriage. I had decided to wed Paulette simply because I am getting old enough that I should be married. There was never any love between us.'

Camilla thought of the moment by the summerhouse, but she held her peace. At the moment it did not matter.

He touched her chin lightly with his finger. 'I have hated the Spanish for what they did to me.'

She voiced a sudden realisation. 'That is also why you have

preyed on British ships; you have sought revenge in that way against your step-brother.'

His silence affirmed her speculation. She studied him. 'You no longer have an English accent.'

'No, I have had to live with Spanish and French at various times. Perhaps now I am thoroughly Americanised.' His eyes lost their hardness and twinkled at the last.

'Jared, who is your step-brother?'

The merriment was gone instantly. 'I have not uttered that man's name in ten years. He is the Earl of Northolt.'

Camilla gasped in surprise.

'I see you must know him.'

She nodded. 'I am so sorry.'

He shrugged. 'It no longer matters. I have gained enough wealth here to make up for what I lost.' He looked at her. 'I suspected you of treachery when you produced Edward Searles; I have not trusted anyone other than myself for all these years.'

'I did not produce him,' she contradicted quietly.

'I realised that finally. I was dreadful; I would not have blamed you had you taken my pistol and shot me that night.' He leaned forward to kiss her lightly once more, then straightened. He released her hands and leaned back in his chair.

'Your dinner will be ice cold,' she said.

His thoughts were elsewhere as he remarked, 'In all fairness, I suppose there is one person I have trusted throughout this time—Etienne,' his eyes shifted to her, 'who is in love with you.'

'I do not think he really is,' she replied. 'How did you and Etienne meet?'

'When I was in bondage to the Spanish, Etienne was brought in from a ship captured by pirates. He was ill and near death, but we became friends and I took him with me when I escaped. He had not fully recovered at the time and has always felt it was an extra burden for me, therefore, I suspect, I earned his undying gratitude.'

'Jared, you will have to tell Paulette.'

'I know, and the sooner the better. I shall go straight from here and tell her that we plan to be wed.'

Camilla remembered the narrowed blue eyes and the emphatic statement declaring that she would allow nothing to interfere with her future as mistress of Belle Havre.

'What are you thinking of?' Jared asked.

She shook her head, not wanting to bring Paulette into their conversation. He turned to eat, then after a few moments he glanced at her. 'Camilla, the British are drawing closer. I would like you to leave until this is over.'

'Not as long as you are here,' she replied.

'Do you realise the odds on this battle? I saw the British troops before I reached Washington last summer. They were organised, armed, dressed in fancy uniforms,' he paused, 'they refer to us as "dirty shirts". They march to battle in straight formal columns which have seen battle before. Jackson cannot hope for many more than two thousand men. Militia from Kentucky and Tennessee are on their way, Hind's Mississippi Dragoons are supposed to be coming.' He stopped a minute to eat, then continued, 'Kentucky is not in this military district, but according to Jackson, the governor of Kentucky has acknowledged his request and is sending the militia.'

'Won't that help?' Camilla asked.

'It would if they arrive in time. On the eighth of December they were at the mouth of the Cumberland River under the command of Major-General John Thomas.

'Thomas notified General Jackson that it would take at least twenty-five days to get as far as Natchez. Major Lacoste, who has a plantation down river, has organised a battalion of free men of colour. Major Villeré is in charge of the Louisiana State Militia. I have volunteered my services as a cannoneer,' he smiled wryly, 'something I learned from privateering.'

She squeezed his arm. 'I shall be so thankful when this is over.'

'Jackson declared martial law in New Orleans on the

sixteenth; notices have been posted all over town.' He studied her and asked, 'Would you rather be in town?'

'Wherever I can be of the most help.'

'Women are forming committees to establish hospitals and collect bed linens, that sort of thing. The legislature has drawn up a measure which grants that no notes or bills of exchange can be collected for one-hundred and twenty days, no property sold during that time, and no civil suit can be filed. All pending suits should cease until May, 1815.'

'The annulment just cleared that law,' Camilla remarked.

'That damn' annulment, I hope we can forget for ever.'

She gazed into his eyes, the love she felt for him welling up within. 'I shall pray for you constantly. I will go to New Orleans if you prefer, and if you think I can be of more help here, I would rather remain at Belle Havre.'

'Promise me, Camilla, if Belle Havre is attacked, you will leave.'

'I promise.'

He regarded her sombrely. 'Camilla, when I arrived home I sent Martin to round up the men. Jackson needs every hand possible. Every able-bodied man on this place who wants to fight will leave; I suspect all will go. My men have too much to lose to not want to fight for it, but that will leave the women here unprotected.'

'I have already promised to go if it becomes necessary,' she answered quietly.

He finished his dinner and leaned back in the chair to consume the last of the wine. 'We are so greatly outnumbered—two thousand men—some have never fought before in their lives, many have no weapons; we are unorganised. We will fight against what may be as many as twelve thousand trained, experienced soldiers.' He smiled at her. 'At least Jackson is willing to have all the help he can get. He has welcomed mine, as well as the Lafittes' and the Baratarians.' He placed his glass on the table and rose to pull her to her feet.

'I shall not engage in smuggling hereafter. That is the last cargo I shall ever bring in under such conditions.'

'Thank goodness!' she said, gazing up at him. He leaned forward and drew her into his arms.

'And I shall fight like hell to get home.' His grey eyes were warm and filled with love. 'This plantation is vastly big enough to supply our needs and occupy my time without privateering and smuggling.'

He released her and grasped her hand. 'I must go.' She walked at his side to the parlour. They entered the darkened room and stood in the shadows while he put his arms around her.

'I will return as soon as I can. At the first sign of danger you are to leave Belle Havre.'

'I have already promised to do so.'

'Aiken is here; he is too old to fight, but I will give him instructions that he is to drive you if you have to leave.'

She nodded, suddenly not trusting herself to speak. Then, realising how little time they had left, she said, 'Jared, you will not be far. If ... if anything happens, come home, please ...'.

He brushed her hair away from her face. 'My darling Camilla, I will not let anything happen to me. Nothing will keep me from returning to you.' He pulled her into his embrace, crushing her against him for a long kiss. Finally he released her and gazed down.

'I must go.' He ran his hand over her cheek and wiped away a tear. 'What is this?' He tilted her face up to his and his voice was tender. 'I thought you never cried,' he teased.

She tried to turn her head. 'I didn't,' she whispered, 'until I met you.'

He lifted her chin and his voice was husky as his eyes went over her face. 'My love, there will not be any more tears when I get home from this.' He kissed her cheek. 'You are a very brave girl.'

She lowered her head. 'Not where you are concerned.'

He crushed her in his arms again and kissed her

passionately until Camilla forgot her tears, forgot the war, or anything except this man whom she loved utterly and completely.

Suddenly he stopped. 'Now, goodbye. You wait right here.'

He was gone in an instant.

Camilla leaned against the wall, feeling the cool plaster against her forehead and listening to the fading clack of his boots against the polished planks in the hall. The door opened and closed and she knew he was gone.

The tears tumbled down her cheeks, burning and dropping across her hands. How long she stood in the darkened room and cried she did not know. Finally she moved away, stepped into the hall and summoned Selena.

The tall black woman faced her with her hands folded over her middle. Camilla said, 'Selena, tomorrow morning we will go into New Orleans; I must see if there is anything I can do to help. I would like you to go with me.'

'Yes ma'am.'

'Selena,' Camilla paused and smiled, 'he has asked me to marry him.'

Selena's face creased in a wide smile. 'Thank the Lord!' she exclaimed.

Camilla reached out and grasped the woman's hands to squeeze them tightly. 'I am so happy, Selena.'

'I am so glad, Mrs Kingston.'

'Oh, how wonderful that sounds. I am not Mrs Kingston yet, Selena, but we will have a wedding.'

'You are Mrs Kingston, ma'am. I'll just call you that right now.'

Camilla laughed. 'It sounds marvellous.' She wished Selena goodnight, but it was only a few short hours until early morning and she rose to talk with the servant once again.

'Selena, gather all the bed-linen we can spare. I want a room prepared here for any sick they might bring to Belle Havre. It will be easier to reach here than New Orleans and we will take in all we can. We will take some of the linens to

town today. Mr Kingston said they are turning homes into
hospitals and I am certain there will be a need for more
bedding.'

'Yes, ma'am,' Selena agreed and hurried to do as
instructed. Camilla gathered her skirts and headed for the
stairs. As long as she could keep busy she would not think so
much about Jared. With all the men gone, Camilla found her
hands full to rearrange many of the duties to keep the plantation functioning at all.

Then, before they could leave for New Orleans, a heavy
rain started and they had to postpone the trip into town. Dry
earth turned to mud, the house grew chilled and the women
servants, as well as Camilla, worked busily.

Three more days passed before Camilla was able to leave
Belle Havre. When she was finally in the carriage settled
opposite Selena, she gazed out at a world vastly different.
Jared had not only taken all the strong young men, but also all
the horses and mules with the exception of two which she
suspected had been left behind for her use if the British came.

The rains had stopped, but mud was still in evidence and
the day was grey and cloudy. When they rode into New
Orleans, Camilla gazed out the carriage window in surprise.
The streets were in chaos. Men were streaming out of town,
some on horseback, some on foot. Women and children lined
the streets and balconies, singing the national anthem of
France, the *Marseillaise,* and *Yankee Doodle.*

There were few uniformed soldiers, not even many
weapons in sight and Camilla recalled Jared's fears. Indians
in buckskins passed, tough flatboatmen, trappers and
farmers.

Camilla saw a familiar face in the throng and ordered Aiken
to turn into a side street and halt. 'I see Mrs Le Meignen in
the crowd. Wait here for me, Selena.'

Without waiting for an answer, Camilla alighted from the
carriage and pushed through the jostling throng until she
reached a line of onlookers at the edge of the street.

'Mrs Le Meignen!' she cried.

The small woman turned, then smiled in recognition. She clasped Camilla's hand and pulled her close. 'Child, have you told your husband goodbye?'

'He left several days ago. What is happening?'

'The British have attacked!' Mrs Le Meignen peered up at Camilla. 'I saw Jared only a few minutes ago.'

Camilla's heart quickened. 'Here?' Her eyes scanned the men pouring down the street. They were dressed in woollen hunting shirts, copperas-dyed pantaloons, raccoon and fox hats, as well as fancy woollen coats and leather breeches.

'Where was Jared, Mrs Le Meignen?'

'At General Jackson's headquarters on Royal Street.'

Camilla thanked her and turned to push her way through the crowd along the *banquette* towards Royal Street. Suddenly a familiar voice called her name.

She whirled to face Jared coming in long strides across the street towards her. He ran and caught her up in a crushing hug which lifted her from the ground, then he released her.

His eyes went past her. 'You are not here alone, are you?'

She shook her head. 'No, Selena is with me. What is happening?'

'The British have commenced the drive for New Orleans. The Villeré family and a small company of militia have been captured; Gabriel Villeré leapt through a window and escaped to tell General Jackson that two thousand British are on his plantation. They will attack in the morning.'

'Jared!' a man called.

He turned and Camilla saw Etienne mounted, waiting with Jared's horse, while the crowd continued to pour past him.

'Jackson has declared we will fight them tonight.' Jared's eyes raked over her features. 'Camilla, I have to leave.' He pulled her to him for one more hard embrace and kissed her hungrily; Camilla clung to him, oblivious of the crowd or proprieties. He released her and went striding for his horse.

Camilla started to move to the edge of the street to watch him go, but she turned slightly and was startled by a pair of blue eyes looking steadfastly at her.

Paulette gazed at her, only yards away, with a smouldering hate which was unmistakable. 'You have lost him to a war,' she hissed.

'Good afternoon, Miss Fourier,' Camilla remarked, not caring to engage in any such conversation. She moved to pass Paulette.

'You will not have him!' The hate in the voice stopped Camilla. Paulette continued, 'I would suggest, Miss Hyde, that you pack your belongings and join your fellow men who are about to attack our city.' Her voice deepened with feeling. 'I will do everything in my power to take him from you!'

Camilla flashed angrily, 'And what about your Frenchman lover?' The instant she had said the words she wished she could take them back.

Paulette's eyes narrowed. 'Have you told Jared?'

Camilla shook her head. 'No. There is no need to.'

'You will never be his wife!'

Camilla did not care to converse with Paulette. She gathered her skirts and swept past her, ignoring the venomous look directed towards her. She waited until Jared's tall figure was out of sight, then returned to her carriage.

'I saw Mr Kingston, Selena. The battle for New Orleans has started; let's leave these things and return home.'

'Yes, ma'am.'

They rode home in thick fog which increased with every passing hour. Camilla sat tensely in the corner of the carriage wondering about the battle that must be taking place down the river from Jared's plantation.

The night was an agony of waiting, then in the early hours she heard horses approaching up the drive and flew to the door.

Jared flung off his horse while Martin and several men galloped past the house towards the stables.

Jared took the steps two at a time and swept her into his arms. He looked down at her and held one arm about her shoulders while they walked into the house together. 'We have fought all through the night, across de la Ronde's plantation as well as Villeré's and Jumonville's. Jackson is moving his army back to Rodriguez Canal between the Chalmette and Macarty plantations.' As he talked he moved in the direction of the library. 'We need some kind of protection—we are going to dig out the old canal for a barricade. The British have stopped fighting temporarily; pray that it gives us time.'

He dropped his arm from around her shoulders and moved to open a tall armoire and lift down all the weapons. 'We need every weapon possible, as well as every spade, shovel and wagon. I am taking all the empty casks to help fill the canal.' He turned and looked at her.

'Camilla, I may not be home now for some time. There are thousands of British soldiers. Let me tell Aiken to take you north, away from this.'

'No, I want to be close to you.'

His arms were full of muskets and flint-locks. He leaned forward to kiss her, then headed for the door. 'I have to leave, everyone is needed. I instructed the men to get all the wagons on the place and to load them with empty barrels and sugar-cakes.'

Camilla asked him to wait and hurried to fetch a hat and cloak. Jared accepted them from her and told her, 'I must see to loading the wagons. We need to hurry.'

'Before you leave stop here again and let me give you food to take.'

He nodded and descended the steps to place the weapons in a wagon which Martin had driven to the front. Camilla hurried inside and called to Selena to see to packing the food. Before she finished with it, Jared appeared once more and announced that he was leaving. He gathered what she had ready and placed it in the wagon; then with one final kiss he was gone. Camilla stood on the steps watching the wagons and carts disappear down the drive, then turned to the house as a deep silence set in.

. . . . .

Christmas came and went with no word from Jared or any of the men. Cold rains plagued them and Camilla prayed that Jared was not having to spend day and night in the mud. Wounded men began to arrive at Belle Havre, and each one that entered caused her heart to beat faster as she searched quickly for Jared.

The pounding of cannon could be heard clearly, and with the returning wounded men came word of the skirmishes. The American schooner, *Carolina*, was blown up and sunk on the twenty-seventh of December. Major-General Thomas's Kentuckians had arrived with few guns. The Choctaws, who could move easily through a swamp, scouted at night, killing any British who came within reach.

On the first day of January the second division of Louisiana Militia arrived from parishes above Baton Rouge, but they had no weapons.

Camilla asked each soldier who came if they knew Jared, or had seen him and on several occasions received word of his well-being. Too late, she learned that a heavy fog on the morning of the first of January prevented fighting and many of the town people joined the men in camp for parades and festivities. She suffered a pang of regret when she was told, wishing that she had been there also.

Then several days passed without any word of Jared. The morning of January the eighth dawned with a thick mist hovering over the ground, and Camilla's spirits sank lower. From all indications, any day they could expect a British assault. There were too many wounded men quartered at Belle Havre now for her to consider leaving.

She moved about her usual tasks and was descending the stairs when Selena came forward. 'Ma'am, there's somebody in the hall to see you.' She lowered her voice and leaned forward. 'He wouldn't say who, Mrs Kingston. Ma'am, he don't look trustworthy.'

'Thank you, Selena, I'll go down.' She descended the stairs and walked forward along the hall. A bearded unkempt man with a bandanna around his head and a gold earring in one ear turned to face her. His dark eyes were small and close-set in a round face above a muscular body clad in a striped shirt and pantaloons which reminded her of the flatboatmen she had seen in New Orleans.

She paused and said, 'I am Miss Hyde.'

'And I'm Bervais. Ma'am,' he lowered his voice, 'Mr Kingston sent me to fetch you. He's been wounded bad, ma'am.'

CHAPTER
TWELVE

'How badly is he hurt?' Camilla asked.

'I dunno, ma'am. If you could come with me ... do you have a carriage? I can drive it. Maybe we could get him home.'

Camilla felt as if she had turned to ice. The room spun and the man's voice seemed to come from far away. 'Of course, let me get some bandages in case ...'

He interrupted. 'Ma'am, I wouldn't take the time. I think we should go.'

'Of course. Let me get my cape.' Selena was no longer in sight, but a young maid stood at the end of the hall. Camilla asked her to fetch a cape and bonnet. Within a moment the girl descended the steps and held out the cape.

The man crossed to the door. 'Ma'am, time's passing.'

Camilla accepted the cape, threw it about her shoulders over her yellow organdy dress, and rushed ahead to lead the way to the stable. She glanced about the yard and asked, 'Did you have a horse?'

'I walked, ma'am,' came his reply.

Camilla was in too much haste to consider his method of arrival, but found Aiken dozing on a bench inside the door with a blanket across his knees to protect him from a chill. Grey fog swirled behind them as they entered, and Camilla roused the old servant.

'Aiken, please hitch the horses. I must go ...' She could not bring herself to say that Jared was wounded. Bervais aided Aiken, then insisted he could drive; soon they were gaining speed as the carriage rushed away from Belle Havre.

The carriage gained a dangerous speed for the rough road with deep ruts after the rains, but Camilla rode inside, unaware and uncaring, wanting only to reach Jared. The fog was as thick and heavy as it had been on her arrival at Belle Havre: she recalled the drive then and thought how long in the past it seemed.

She gazed at the thick grey vapour outside the carriage. Out of its opacity the tall pillars which marked the entrance to Belle Havre appeared. They turned to travel up the River Road, towards New Orleans, and Camilla noticed their direction with surprise. She thought all the fighting had been below, farther along to the south from Belle Havre.

Within a short time they turned again; Camilla lost all sense of direction. She did not know where they were, much less the direction of their destination. The mist hid everything from view until they were within a few yards of any object. No cannon sounded, nor any commotion from fighting. How badly was he hurt? Camilla asked herself this question over and over. She closed her eyes, doubling her hands into fists in her lap while she prayed silently that it was not serious.

The ride seemed interminable; finally the carriage bounced violently a short distance, then halted, and within seconds Bervais opened the door.

Camilla climbed out and gazed about in surprise. She could see only a few feet in the fog and early morning greyness, but the sounds were unmistakable, recalling the same noises she had listened to all the time she had resided in Boisblanc's cabin. Frogs croaked in a steady rhythmical noise. They were on the edge of a swamp.

She turned to the swarthy heavy-set man waiting for her. 'Where are we?'

'This way, ma'am. We need to ride in a pirogue, a swamp-boat, to reach him. You must be careful.'

Suddenly Camilla had a strange sense of doom, a rising feeling of something being wrong. 'Where is Mr Kingston?'

'He's on the other side of the swamp. This will be the quickest way to reach him.'

'I don't hear any fighting.'

'No, ma'am. There's been a lull since yesterday.'

'I will wait and you bring him here,' Camilla stated, not knowing why she said it. Suddenly she felt she did not want to be alone with this man who called himself Bervais. She took a step back away from him, but the dark eyes remained on her in an impassive fixed stare.

'Ma'am, I'd hate to get over there and have something happen to him before I could get him back here. He asked for you over and over.'

Camilla shrugged away the feeling in a quick longing for Jared. 'Very well.'

Bervais sounded relieved. 'Let me take your hand. I'll steady the pirogue; these are tricky.'

Camilla allowed him to take her hand. She felt the powerful muscles tense as he helped her into the boat, rather like an English punt. He moved to the end and sat facing her, then lifted a pole to push into the water.

They began to move through the waters soundlessly; Camilla knew she was with a swamp man. The fog did nothing to help her feelings; it curled eerily above the shimmering black water. She pulled the cape tighter about her shoulders. 'Where is he wounded?' she asked, her own voice sounding unnaturally loud in the silence.

'Where?' Bervais repeated her question.

There was a moment's silence. She urged him to answer. 'Yes, where?'

'He was fighting over there on the other side of the swamp.'

Once again she had a deep feeling that something was amiss. Bervais had strange answers to her questions. 'I meant, where is he hurt, in the leg?'

'Oh, aye, in the leg and the shoulder.'

The answer came quickly and Camilla felt absolutely certain that the man was lying. But why would he? What purpose would he have? She frowned slightly, staring across the length of the boat at his expressionless face. 'Has he bled much?'

'Terribly.'

Camilla did not know what was happening, but she suspected that Bervais was anything but what he had said. Why would he come to Belle Havre and entice her away on a pretext? It made no sense, yet she remained certain he was lying about something. And if so . . . She gazed about her; every second they were plunging deeper and deeper into the swamp.

Bervais had put away the pole and was using an oar, dipping it steadily into the water to paddle with the slightest ripple each time he raised it. Somewhere nearby a bird cried in a high warbling sound which was sad and forlorn in the silence.

The long grey moss hung from cypress limbs above them, visible only when the boat passed close at hand, then fading to be swallowed once more in mist. Camilla glanced at Bervais. He watched her in a steady unblinking stare. If he was not taking her to Jared, then what was he doing?

She clutched the sides of the narrow boat. 'Where are we going? I insist on an answer?'

'I am taking you into the swamp.'

'I want to return to the carriage.'

He continued to paddle silently and ignored her request. She looked over her shoulder. The mist closed in behind them revealing only the trees near the boat. Left on her own she would have no way of knowing which direction to take. A rising panic gripped her as she faced him and insisted, 'I want to return to the carriage!'

He did not answer; Camilla suddenly was overwhelmed with fright at being in the swamp. She untied the bonnet and flung it in the murky waters in a futile gesture, as if the hat would be a marker.

He laughed. ' 'Twill do you no good. You could throw your whole dress over and no one would ever know.'

With a sinking heart Camilla knew what he said was true, but even worse, from his reaction she realised that her feelings about him had been correct. He had some evil intention. 'Is Jared hurt?' she asked.

'I have no idea.'

The only thing she could feel was relief. Jared was all right! 'Thank heaven!' she breathed. She regarded Bervais. 'Where are you taking me? And why?'

'I am not supposed to tell you,' he replied.

'I shall know soon enough, so what will it matter if I know right now?' she persisted.

He rowed in silence, then finally spoke. 'I am to take you into the swamp and kill you.'

She gasped and gripped the boat tighter. 'Kill me!' She stared in disbelief. He had uttered it in complete calm and continued to row with dreadful purpose. 'But why?' she cried. 'Who would want you to do such a thing?'

He shrugged. 'I cannot tell.'

She gazed at him feeling perplexed and terrified. 'You surely cannot intend to do this!'

Again his indifferent voice replied, 'I am paid well.'

'But you will hang for it!'

He laughed in a harsh nasal sound. 'Never! People disappear in these swamps and are never seen again. No one will ever know—'gators, that sort of thing. I have nothing to fear.'

Camilla shivered and pulled her cape closer under her chin. 'If I do not have long to live, what difference will it make if I know who is behind this?'

He did not answer, but continued to paddle silently, the oar rising and dipping into the water. Finally he replied, 'Guess it don't matter none. Miss Fourier don't want you around her man.'

Camilla closed her eyes as if she could shut out the nightmare of his declaration. She opened them in a moment and looked at the mist floating over the water, then down into that terrible blackness. Her mind began to race over any possibilities of saving herself. She had to struggle to speak in a normal tone of voice. 'How far will you row?'

He chuckled, a throaty sound of cunning satisfaction. 'Well, now, Mrs Kingston . . .'

Camilla interrupted, 'I am not presently "Mrs Kingston".'

He shrugged. 'You were, and that's sufficient. You're a real pretty lady. Seems a waste and a shame to take such a pretty gal out into a dark old swamp and feed her to the 'gators.'

He chuckled again. Camilla clung to the sides of the pirogue. 'What are you going to do?'

'I have a cabin, way out here in the swamp; it's hidden and no one knows about it, 'cept a chum or two. I keep things out here. I'm gonna let you come live with me.'

Another wave of faintness washed over her. She fought it down and stared at him. 'You can't do such a thing!'

He grinned, a malicious smirk which revealed broken teeth. 'I can, Mrs Kingston. It's the easiest thing in the world.'

She feared his words were true. She longed for the safety of Jared's presence, but he was away, fighting for New Orleans. No one would know where she was. She had left Belle Havre without informing anyone of what she was doing. She had told Aiken she was leaving and he had helped hitch the horses to the carriage, but she did not tell him why. How long would it be before anyone noticed her absence and began to look for her? She remembered the carriage then, at the edge of the swamp. She glanced at her captor. 'They will be searching for me shortly.'

'Won't matter none,' he replied. 'No one will find you.'

'But if you hold me prisoner, you won't be able to leave, to go to New Orleans. I would escape.'

Again she heard his sly laugh. 'I can go any time I get a notion. You won't leave. You couldn't find your way out of here if I gave you a boat and paddle. And the swamp is full of critters that would snap up a tender morsel like you, Mrs

Kingston. They'd do it right quick. Water moccasins, 'gators. No, you won't be leaving—not of your own accord.'

'Jared will kill you,' she stated, and for the first time when he answered the certainty was gone from his voice.

'He won't ever know.'

There was no answer to that. She knew he spoke the truth. Jared would never know what had happened to her, or that Paulette was behind it. 'He will realise that I was taken away from Belle Havre; Aiken and our people will give him a description of you.'

'I ain't worried. There are a hundred men around here who fit that description. People have disappeared around these parts since the town started. There are whispers and rumours, but no one ever knows what happened.'

He rowed a moment, then spoke with a growl, 'Mrs Kingston, I don't want to hear any more about your husband. A cannon ball may relieve me of concern about him anyway. I don't like the arrogant gentleman any, so kindly shut your mouth.'

Camilla realised that she was making the man nervous with thoughts of Jared. She declared with firmness, 'He is a deadly marksman, and he will never stop searching for me.'

Bervais' hand shot out and clamped around her wrist. He twisted it painfully until Camilla cried out, then released her. 'Mrs Kingston, you're going to have to do as I say.'

She rubbed her wrist; tears stung her eyelids. She blinked them away and rode in silence. All too clearly she saw the extent of her dilemma. The only hope she had of someone finding her was the carriage at the edge of the swamp. Perhaps he would forget about it.

She stared down at the black water. Perhaps it would be better to jump out of the pirogue to try to escape now, before he had her in a cabin. She would rather die in the swamp than be forced to live with such a creature. She hesitated in indecision. 'Where are we? It cannot hurt for me to know.'

'We're in the middle of a swamp and you can't ever leave it

alive.' He grinned at her. ''Course, as long as you're good company, Mrs Kingston, I'll keep you around.'

She understood clearly what he was implying. 'If Miss Fourier ever discovers you went against her wishes, she will have you killed.' Camilla knew no such thing about Paulette, but merely said it to attempt to disturb her captor.

'I ain't worried none about that. I can handle Miss Fourier.'

He remained calm and Camilla understood why. He had everything as it suited him. No one would find her. She would have to decide between dying in the swamp, or living with the dreadful man.

She rode with all feeling gone. How foolish she had been and so easy to trick—as Paulette must have known she would be with her love for Jared. She had not questioned Bervais' motives or his identity; she had made no precautions for her own protection and safety, and now she would have to pay for the blunder with her life.

The pirogue glided out from beneath a thick stand of cypress into a clearing. The water was calm with the mist hovering above it, parting as their boat sliced through the vapour until it rolled away to reveal a shack resting on a small island of shells. Behind and to one side of the structure which was built on stilts, were cypress hung with moss; the shack had a high sloping roof which angled over a narrow porch.

Camilla eyed it with dread as the pirogue drifted to bump gently against a plank walk which ran from the porch across a short stretch of shells and into the water for several yards.

Bervais clambered on to the walk causing the pirogue to rock wildly; for an instant Camilla was tempted to throw herself into the water, anything to escape remaining with him, but he reached down and caught her arm leaving her no choice. He lifted her out on to the walk and pulled her close

CHAPTER
THIRTEEN

CAMILLA struggled to pull her arms free of his grasp as he yanked her close to kiss her. She attempted to turn her head away. 'Let me go!' she cried.

He caught her chin and forced her face to his, placing his mouth on hers and kissing her. He released her, and Camilla stepped away feeling sick with revulsion. She wiped her mouth with her hand.

He laughed harshly. 'You'll change, Mrs Kingston.'

She looked up at him and pleaded, 'Please, whatever Miss Fourier is paying you, Mr Kingston will pay you more.'

'That husband of yours would slit my throat before I got the words out of my mouth.'

'Don't be ridiculous! Not if you had a pistol.'

'I'd as soon stick my head in a 'gator's mouth. I wouldn't face him with a brace of pistols. I got more sense than that.'

Camilla begged with desperation, 'Please, I am wealthy—allow me to pay you. He will not even know about it. I will pay you whatever sum you ask. Surely one woman would not be worth all the money you want?'

He stared at her and rubbed his chin thoughtfully, then shook his head. 'That sounds tempting, Mrs Kingston, but there would be no way to get the money to me without it being discovered that I'm holding you here.'

'Please ... surely there is some way.'

'No. 'Tis too risky.' He climbed down into the pirogue once more.

'Are you leaving?' she asked in surprise.

'Yes, I can't leave the carriage right out in plain sight.'

Her sense of hopelessness mounted. 'What will you do with it?'

'Load it with rocks and sink it in the swamp.'

'It is worth a lot,' Camilla reminded him.

'So is my life,' he replied. He lifted a paddle and began to push away from the walk.

She stepped to the edge of the rough boards and gazed down at him. 'What about the horses?'

'Kill 'em, feed them to the 'gators.'

Jared's beautiful horses. Camilla stared at him, then remarked, 'Those horses are excellent stock, Bervais. They would bring a handsome price.'

He glanced up at her and she guessed that the thought had occurred to him. She continued to press her point, 'They are magnificent animals; you are going to be slaughtering something that could bring you more than Miss Fourier is paying.'

He rowed without a word, but Camilla hoped he was considering what she said. The gap between the pirogue and the walk widened while the mists surrounded the small craft. She turned away and walked towards the cabin to get out of his view.

The interior of the shack called to mind Boisblanc's rough cabin. While both were crudely constructed, Boisblanc's had been clean and tidy; this one was littered with a foul putrid odour of fish, rotten food, and sweat. Camilla gazed around the darkened interior in a growing determination to do anything to protect herself from Bervais when he returned. She walked slowly around the room which contained a makeshift bed constructed from cypress logs and rushes which smelled sour, and caused her to hold her skirts close as she passed it.

A table and wooden chairs were in the centre of the room. Food and dirty utensils were strewn across the top; a mouse scampered across the floor at her approach.

She remembered Boisblanc's collection of weapons. Surely one who lived in such a manner as Bervais would be armed too! She looked about her and saw a trunk at one end of the bed.

Camilla tugged at the lid and found it locked. She located a bar on the floor under the table. The lock was old and flimsy, but with a steady pounding it soon came free. She raised the lid to find a collection of knives and dismantled flint-locks. She selected one knife, then in a swift motion scooped up the remaining weapons, carried them down to the end of the plank walk and dropped them in the water, knowing all the time that she would gain nothing by the gesture but his anger.

She paused on the walk to gaze at her surroundings. The mists were thinning and she could see more clearly. To her right were live oaks, but it would be impossible to hide among them. Within minutes he could search the entire area.

She stared into the dark water at her feet. It appeared greenish brown, opaque and glistening, hiding any life which teemed below its surface. The thought of alligators and snakes was unpleasant.

She shivered at the consideration of the possibilities, none of which were desirable, but she refused to wait and do nothing until he returned.

She returned to the shack, aware of the passage of time. Bervais would not be gone long if he decided to kill the horses. In futility she looked about. There was nothing to defend herself with sufficiently; she had no illusions as to how much protection the knife would be against Bervais' strength.

She lighted a candle to see better, but gained nothing from a second search of the shack. She glanced in the direction of the water fearfully, as if expecting him to appear at any moment, then turned and stared at the small flickering candlelight.

An idea came; it would gain her little, but at least there would be no shack for him to hide and keep her prisoner inside. With haste she gathered all the rags and clothing she could find, anything she could burn, and piled them on the bed.

She tipped the candle and held the flame to the pile to light the sleeve of a frayed black shirt. The material caught, smouldered and curled as a thin line of fire spread, then flamed. She shifted the candle to light another place, then one more, until all burned intensely.

The flames leapt high, curling up the wall and heating the small space. The rush bed caught with a whoosh which caused Camilla to jump back from its flame.

While the black smoke mushroomed and caused her eyes to sting, she gathered what she could find to make another small bundle of trash on the table. Covering her mouth with her hand, Camilla waited until that, too, caught and burned.

She stumbled from the shack, choking and coughing from the smoke, then paused to light one more fire on the porch. As soon as this was completed she fled towards the giant oaks at the other end of the tiny island.

Breathing deeply of the fresh air, she gazed out over the water but did not see any sign of Bervais; she shifted her glance to observe the burning shack.

The roof was ablaze with orange flames leaping high, while smoke from inside billowed through the opening. Gradually tongues of flame licked across the porch and caught the plank walk.

Cinders and red sparks shot upwards as the entire shack blazed, with thick black smoke rolling upwards, then spreading in a dark cloud above the swamp.

A deep hollow rumble came from the conflagration; the bright flames reflected across the water in a shimmering redness. Even across the short distance to the trees she felt the heat.

Camilla watched across the open water for Bervais' approach, which would be easy to see now that the morning mists were gone. She looked down at her hand; she still clutched the knife tightly, although she suspected it would never be of use to her.

A movement caught her eye, and the pirogue slid into sight from the depths of the cypress' shadows. She stepped behind the huge trunk of an oak and peered cautiously around to watch Bervais.

He paddled furiously and her fear mounted at his approach. His eyes rolled wildly over the destruction. The pirogue slid towards the island, but before it stopped he sprang from the boat and ran towards the fire, bellowing in rage.

Her heart throbbed violently as she feared he had taken leave of his senses. He ran to and fro in front of the flames, beating at them with his bandanna in complete ineffectualness.

Loud cries of rage and frustration came from him; Camilla knew he would destroy her as soon as he found her. She stared at the pirogue, abandoned and wallowing in the water at the edge of the island.

If she could reach the pirogue and slip away while his attention was on the fire, at least she would be free of harm from him. Even if she could not find her way out of the swamp, she would be safe for the time being.

She eyed the small boat as her only hope, but to reach it she would have to cross an open stretch of island within a few yards of Bervais.

He continued to race back and forth hitting at the flames and shouting angrily. There was nothing to be gained from waiting. She caught her skirts in her hand and ran for the pirogue.

Her heart pounded painfully as she ran; she plunged into the ankle deep water and caught the pirogue to shove it away from the island. Too terrified to look back, she dropped the knife inside, then scrambled in behind it and yanked up the paddle to row.

She had no sooner dipped the oar into water than he turned and saw her. For one dreadful moment they looked into each other's eyes.

CHAPTER
FOURTEEN

SHE plunged the paddle into the water and pulled with all her strength, lifting and dipping it rapidly, while she watched him in terror.

The moment he turned and saw her, Bervais began running for the pirogue. He waved his arms in anger and bellowed furiously at her.

The boat cut through the water and gained speed; the distance between the island and the craft increased, then Camilla watched in horror as he unhesitatingly charged into the water after her. Within seconds he caught the end of the boat and held it fast. Never in her life had she seen such fury in a human. She scrambled to get out of the pirogue and fled from him in any way possible.

Bervais stood in chest-deep water. He reached out and caught her arm in a crushing grip and flung her down in the pirogue.

Camilla reached for the knife which lay on the bottom of the boat, but as fast as her fingers closed over its hilt he yanked her wrist up in a painful twist and she dropped it with a cry.

His hands closed around her throat and she tugged against them. 'I will kill you for this!' he yelled.

She gasped, 'The smoke! They will find . . . you!'

She struggled to break free of his murderous grip. The world darkened, then suddenly he released her. He climbed into the boat while Camilla gasped for air.

Her throat ached, as well as her wrist, but she realised he must have heeded her words. For a moment he sat and glared at the dying fire; the shack was now a charred blackened ruin which smouldered and smoked. The plank wall had crumbled and fallen into the swamp except for the part near the porch which was black in contrast to the ground and lay in burning pieces.

Bervais swore and turned to stare at her. 'I shall kill you for this! You will regret this a thousand times before I am through with you.'

He took up the paddle and began to row, never taking his eyes from her.

There was no need to answer him, and she sat in silence. Her hair had come unpinned and hung over her shoulders. The cape was wet and clung damply around her ankles. She unfastened it and let it drop to the seat. The skirt of her yellow organdy dress was also wet, and she leaned forward to squeeze the water from its folds.

The knife lay in the bottom of the boat where she had dropped it, but it was useless to reach for it. He would only hurt her once more.

Bervais rowed steadily; his boots, grey pantaloons and even his striped shirt were wet. If it caused him any discomfort he gave no indication, but stared at her with malevolence.

Finally she saw the bank. The horses were tethered under the trees, but there was no sign of the carriage. The minute he stopped she scrambled out of the pirogue quickly, then ran for her life.

She dashed ahead of him to reach the horses, then raced on past them, deciding it would take too long to get them untied. She followed a narrow path as she ran between the huge oaks.

Bervais caught her easily. His hand clamped on her shoulder and spun her about. He slapped her in anger, then grabbed her wrist to pull her along beside him while he returned to the horses. He held fast to her arm and stepped to retrieve the knife from the pirogue, then turned and lifted her easily on to the back of one of the horses.

He took the reins and held them while he mounted the other horse, then turned and faced her.

'You cannot escape; don't try again. I'm taking you to my place in New Orleans. We will ride near town, then wait until dark so no one will see us. We have to cross the road; don't try to get help if we meet someone.' Bervais held up the knife. 'I will slit the throat of anybody who attempts to help you or interferes with me.' He reached out to twist her arm cruelly. 'Do you understand, Mrs Kingston?'

She cried out in pain, then answered him, and he released her. He stared at her, his small eyes filled with fury. 'You will be sorry for what you've done,' he stated. He turned his horse, still holding the reins to hers to lead the way.

They headed away from the swamp. Camilla glanced over her shoulder and saw her cape still lying in the pirogue. Either he was certain that no one would find it, or he had stopped thinking logically about his actions.

It little mattered at the moment, because it appeared hopeless even if the cape was left behind. She glanced about her, deciding to try once more before they reached New Orleans to get away from him.

She stared at Bervais' broad back; if he would continue to ride in front there might come a moment when she could slip away. Her throat and arm both ached from his brutality, and she knew that once he had her alone he would be merciless.

They headed away from the swamp, but had gone only a short distance when they heard hoofbeats approaching. Bervais turned quickly. 'Someone is coming!' He led her horse into a thicket and ordered her to dismount. 'Do not run away; I can find you anywhere here, and if you make a sound I will kill whoever is coming. Do you understand?'

She nodded. He took her horse with him as he rode away. A man spoke loudly. 'Bervais! We've been searching for you.' The voice, which was high and filled with fear, grew louder.

'What do you want with me?' Bervais grumbled.

Camilla longed to cry out, but she remembered his threat and held her peace. She turned to get away while she had a chance, having no intention of standing silently until he returned. She took a step, then stopped instantly at the sound of another man speaking.

Jared Kingston asked, 'Where is Miss Hyde?'

Before Bervais could speak the other man said, 'He made me bring him out here, Bervais! He's been looking all over New Orleans for you, and he made me tell him.'

'Shut up!' Bervais growled. 'I don't know what you're talking about,' he replied to Jared.

Camilla wanted to run to Jared, he was only yards away, yet she remembered that long knife and Bervais's threat. She had no way of knowing if Jared was armed or not; she could not put him in danger of a surprise assault by Bervais if he was defenceless. She waited and listened.

'I think you know full well,' Jared stated. His voice was low. 'Where is she?'

'I have no idea,' Bervais replied.

'You are riding my horse and leading another from my stable,' Jared declared.

Bervais answered with surprise. 'I can't be! I bought these animals only an hour ago from a man along the road.'

Camilla parted the branches slightly, attempting to get a view. Jared said, 'You are lying! Where is she? What have you done to her?'

Camilla moved a branch and could see them. Bervais was seated, facing Jared and another man. Jared was dressed in buckskins and no weapon was in sight. Bervais faced her direction while Jared was half turned away from her; if she stepped out of hiding, Bervais would see her first.

Jared's voice was cold. 'Bervais, I have talked with Miss Fourier. She admitted everything and told me you had taken Miss Hyde with you. What have you done to her?'

Camilla cried out suddenly, no longer able to stand keeping quiet. 'Jared! He has a knife!'

Instantly Bervais whipped out the knife and leapt at Jared. Just as rapidly Jared drew a pistol and fired.

While the explosion reverberated in the air, the man beside Jared kicked his horse and galloped away.

Camilla pushed through the branches ignoring their sharp points which scraped her skin. As she ran towards them Bervais went limp and toppled to the ground, then lay still.

Instantly Jared leapt from the horse and ran to catch Camilla in his arms and crush her to him. She clung to him and turned her face up to his; he leaned down to kiss her, then finally released her slightly.

'I was afraid I had come too late,' he said in a husky voice, and pulled her against him once more.

After a moment he asked, 'Did he hurt you?'

She gazed up solemnly. 'Not really.'

'His friend said he had a shack in the swamp. When we were coming we saw smoke and . . .' he breathed deeply. 'I could not get here fast enough . . .'

'I burned his place.'

'The devil!' He grinned suddenly. 'Perhaps you did not need me . . .'

'Oh, no!' she interrupted. All the horror and fright she had just experienced welled up in her and she tightened her arms around his neck as she flung herself against him.

His arms closed tightly about her and he held her close. 'My love,' he whispered, 'how I prayed you would be all right.'

She felt the rough buckskin under her cheek and listened to his heart beating steadily. His clothes reeked of leather and gunpowder. Finally she raised her head. 'How did you know what had happened?'

'I will tell you,' he glanced at the still form of Bervais, 'but first I must see to this.' He crossed and knelt to touch Bervais' body, then looked up at her. 'He is dead.'

The body was sprawled on the ground, a dark stain of blood where he had been shot in the chest. Camilla met Jared's eyes. 'What do we do now?'

He mounted, then lifted her up before him. 'I will see you home safely, then take care of this matter.'

He turned the horse to head for the road. Camilla asked, 'Who was the man with you?'

Jared gave a dry humourless laugh. 'One of the deceased's friends.'

'I never expected to see you; I thought you were away fighting,' Camilla said.

His voice was filled with triumph. 'We won!'

She looked up in surprise. 'Won? Do you mean the fighting is over?'

'For all practical purposes it is over.'

She studied him. 'I cannot believe the fight for New Orleans is finished.'

'The Battle of New Orleans was ended this morning.' He stared over her head into space. 'Early this morning, Jackson received reports of the enemy advancing in force, but the mist prevented visibility of anything beyond a few hundred yards. The British were under the command of Wellington's brother-in-law, Major General Sir Edward Pakenham.' He looked down at her. 'Camilla, we were dug in the mud, facing the British. They came marching forward in those bright red coats, in some cases they were sixty abreast, walking into our fire. Pakenham was killed, his second-in-command, Major-General Samuel Gibbs, was slain. Within twenty-five minutes after the battle had commenced the main British commanders were killed or wounded and out of battle.'

'Did they surrender?'

'No, scattered fighting continued, but for the most part it is over. A truce was agreed upon, the British requested it to bury their dead and Jackson agreed. He has detailed men to help the British gather up the wounded and dead. So far, when I left, I knew of only five Americans killed.' He glanced down at her. 'I am certain there will be over a thousand British casualties at least.'

'I pray that is the end,' Camilla said.

'All that magnificent army with its superior military commanders,' Jared mused, 'defeated in such a short time by backwoodsmen, swamp men, men with aged weapons and no training ...' His voice trailed off for a moment, then he added, 'Jackson deserves a great deal of credit.

He has made Americans out of a motley background of nationalities.'

'Why did you leave?'

He looked down at her and pulled a strand of hair away from her face. 'After the battle I knew I would not be needed for a time; Belle Havre is not that far from the fighting. Too damn' close, as a matter of fact. I had hoped you were in New Orleans.' He sounded amused as he added, 'I am certain you would never do anything that uncomplicated.'

She looked up and saw the twinkle in his eyes. 'You have not answered my question.'

'I came home to see you,' he replied, then sobered. 'It is a good thing I did. You were gone; first Selena told me about Bervais, then Aiken.'

'How did you know where to look for me?'

'You know few people around here, and fortunately, Etienne . . .' He paused and groaned aloud. 'I completely forgot Etienne!'

'What did you forget?' she asked.

'He is searching in New Orleans for you. I will have to find him. I will send someone from Belle Havre to look for him.'

'Jared, will you please tell me what you did!'

'As I said, fortunately Etienne was with me, so that eliminated any question of you leaving over something concerning him.'

'When I considered all those people you know, it was easy to narrow it down quickly,' his voice hardened, 'and I went to Paulette first.'

He looked down at her and his arms tightened. 'Camilla, I am sorry. I feel responsible, because she never would have attempted such a thing if I had not given her reason to think . . .'

Camilla reached up and placed her fingers against his lips. 'Please, Jared, that is not necessary.'

'She wanted Belle Havre, Camilla. It did not take long for me to wring the truth out of her. Her father knows it all now. As soon as she told me about Bervais, Etienne and I split up and began to search for his friends. I found that fellow and he told me Bervais had a shack in the swamp. I persuaded him to show me the way—and you know the rest. The law will take care of Paulette.'

'It is over now. I did not stop to think about anything when he told me you had been injured. It wasn't until we were in the pirogue in the swamp that I began to suspect he was not telling the truth. He said he was supposed to kill me, but he was taking me to that shack to live with him because he told me no one would ever know.'

Jared swore under his breath. Camilla continued, 'He left the carriage at the edge of the swamp and took me to his shack, then went back to get rid of the carriage.'

Jared groaned, 'Have I lost a carriage?'

'I suspect it has been filled with rocks and sunk in the swamp.'

'Did you set fire to his place while he was disposing of my carriage?'

'Yes, I couldn't think of anything to do. It was back in the swamp located on a small island. I didn't want to wait and do nothing.'

'I am certain of that.'

She glanced up. 'You are laughing at me again!'

'My Camilla . . .' he leaned down and kissed her hungrily. 'I have been so worried about you.' He held her tightly. 'We could see the smoke almost from the time we left town. What happened then?'

'He returned and went crazy over the fire. I tried to slip past him and get to the pirogue, but he caught me. He was . .' Her voice faded at the last and she turned her head against his chest.

Jared reached down to press his hand against her head winding his fingers in her hair. 'This seems the most natural place for you to be—before me on a horse. Perhaps for our honeymoon we should take one horse and journey . . .'

Camilla looked up at him, then both of them laughed. She wrapped her arms around his neck and smiled up at him. After a moment she asked, 'How long will you be home?'

'I will have to return tonight, Camilla, but I will ask General Jackson. I have a strong feeling that I will be home permanently within a day or two.'

'How good that sounds! Jared, I have turned two rooms over for the sick and wounded.'

'That's good,' he replied and listened while she told him what had transpired in his absence, and of preparations for her wedding gown.

Finally they turned in the drive for Belle Havre; when they reached the house Camilla looked at Jared. 'I am so thankful to be home.'

He kissed her once more, then helped her down. 'I will be back as soon as possible.' He turned and rode away while she stood on the steps and watched until he was lost from sight.

Camilla stood on the upstairs gallery and watched the drive for sign of her husband's return. Early spring flowers dotted the lawn in front of the house, and a light breeze caught the ruffles of her white organdy dress. Then, between the oaks, she saw the phaeton approaching. She turned and ran inside to descend the stairs and hurry to the front.

Within minutes Jared's booted feet sounded in the hall. He entered, his grey eyes lighting at the sight of her. He crossed to her in swift strides, caught her hand, and pulled her into the parlour.

With a swift movement he kicked the door shut behind him and swept her into his arms. His mouth came down on hers in a lingering passionate kiss, then he raised his head to look at her. ' 'Tis the first time we have been separated since we returned from our honeymoon, and it seemed for ever instead of mere hours.'

She laughed and gazed at him, running her fingers through his thick brown hair. 'I have been watching for you to return.'

He smiled and took her hand, then crossed to the sofa t

pull her on to his lap. Camilla glanced at the door in alarm.
'Jared, suppose Selena should come in?'

'There is no danger of that; the door is closed.'

She smiled and said, 'I received a letter from Mrs Madison
today, and Aberdine is on her way here. Now, what has
happened while we were gone?'

She smoothed the collar of his pale green coat, then rested
her hands against his white shirt. She could feel a vibration in
his chest when he talked.

'Etienne will call soon, all is well with him. I was besieged
with invitations, and you will commence having ladies call
tomorrow morning.'

'And I will not be alone with you half as much,' she
declared. She ran her finger along his jaw. Gone was the
beard; his skin was tanned and clean-shaven.

'Camilla, it has taken so long for word to reach here, but
the war with England was over before we fought the Battle of
New Orleans.'

She gasped and stared at him in surprise. 'Then it was all in
vain! How dreadful!'

'No, my dearest, I do not think it was for nought. We
gained a unity of spirit here that the people of New Orleans
had not held before.' He paused for a moment, then added,
'Many British have stayed on here to live, some of their
wounded are still here.' His eyes rested on her. 'Also, today I
have heard at long last from your solicitor.' Jared grinned
wickedly at her. 'I see you had no cause to marry me for my
wealth.'

She regarded him with a smile. 'A fact of which I informed
you on more than one occasion.'

'Now, the question is—what do you want to do with your
home in England?'

She became solemn. 'I have given thought to it. Unless
there is some reason for you to want otherwise—my home is
here.'

'My love . . .' he breathed and pulled her to him. His lips
were warm, demanding on hers.

Camilla entwined her arms about his neck and clung to him, turning against him and responding to his touch with joy.

He shifted and lowered her against the sofa pillows, all the while kissing her. He raised above her slightly to look down at her, and Camilla gazed into his grey eyes with rapture. His voice was deep as he spoke.

'I love you . . .' He leaned down to kiss her once again, his mouth tender on hers, promising a life of joy and love.

Masquerade
Historical Romances

Intrigue excitement romance

Don't miss
February's
other enthralling Historical Romance title

LADY OF STARLIGHT
by Margot Holland

When the warrior King William I comes to visit her
father's castle with his train of nobles, Lady Alyce
de Beaumont — as lovely and impulsive as she is
young and untried — is overwhelmed by William's
power . . . and by the charm of Roger de Boveney,
one of his knights.

Though he and his brother Gilbert look almost
identical, Alyce cannot understand how anyone
could confuse two such different men. Certainly the
coldly aloof Gilbert has saved her from the brutal
lust of a neighbouring Count, but it is Roger who
swears he loves her and gets the King's consent to
marry her. And having accepted him, why should
Alyce still doubt which brother has won her heart?

Masquerade
Historical Romances

Intrigue excitement romance

CHANGE OF HEART
by Margaret Eastvale

Edmund, Lord Ashorne, returned from the Peninsular Wars to find that his fiancée had married his cousin. It was her sister Anne who had remained single for his sake!

LION OF LANGUEDOC
by Margaret Pemberton

Accused of witchcraft by Louis XIV's fanatical Inquisitor, Marietta was rescued by Léon de Villeneuve — the Lion of Languedoc. How could she *not* fall in love with him, even knowing that he loved another woman?